CALL ME LIZZY

Mary T. Wilkinson

CALL ME LIZZY

TATE PUBLISHING
AND ENTERPRISES, LLC

Published by Tate Publishing & Enterprises, LLC
127 E. Trade Center Terrace | Mustang, Oklahoma 73064 USA
1.888.361.9473 | www.tatepublishing.com

Tate Publishing is committed to excellence in the publishing industry. The company reflects the philosophy established by the founders, based on Psalm 68:11,
"The Lord gave the word and great was the company of those who published it."

Book design copyright © 2014 by Tate Publishing, LLC. All rights reserved.
Cover design by Nikolai Purpura
Interior design by Joana Quilantang

Published in the United States of America

ISBN: 978-1-62994-627-6
1. Fiction / Christian / General
2. Fiction / Family Life
13.12.10

This book is dedicated to Phyllis Riley, whose true life story was the spark of inspiration for this fictitious one, and to my husband, Paul, who is my biggest fan and the love of my life.

ACKNOWLEDGEMENTS

I'd like to thank my Lord, Jesus Christ, for giving me the desire to tell stories from the time I was a young girl. I want this book to give Him glory. Appreciation goes out to my Indiana Writing Project Fellows, from Ball State University, for pushing me to get my stories on paper. I also want to thank my sister, Debbie Thomas, for being my cheerleader and mentor in trusting God to turn those words into a published work. Finally, to all of my twelve siblings, I say thanks for the encouragement you have always given me and for lifting me up in prayer over this book. God heard and answered those prayers. He said, "Yes!"

CHAPTER 1

"Cheer up, little Lizzy," Grandpa Roy said pulling gently on my red braids. He was hoping to get a smile out of me. "You might break a gasket if you keep frowning like that." I wasn't amused. When your grandpa is retired from a car factory, you get used to everything he says revolving around car parts. Knowing that I was his little Lizzy comforted me, but my heart was breaking too badly to smile.

"You've got to get your mind off of it and get on with life, Lizzy Girl," he reminded me. "Your parents are the ones who made the mistake, not you."

I wanted to believe I wasn't to blame, but when your parents are getting divorced, you always wonder if somehow it was your fault.

Daddy had been laid off from the factory for six months and couldn't seem to get a job. He and mom were fighting constantly. He said she drank too much, and she said he was a bum.

"I've reenlisted in the army," Daddy had announced just last week. "They promised me I'd see the world, and I'm going to take them up on it. I'll send you home enough money to support your habit."

"And what am I supposed to do; be a single mom cooped up here at home just waiting for you to come back?" Mom had screamed back at him. "Before I met you, I was going to be an actress. If you go back into the service, then I'm going to New York."

I sat in the corner in the overstuffed chair, trying to make myself smaller, as they continued to argue, especially when my name came up in the conversation.

"Do whatever you want," he said. "You always do anyway, but I don't want you taking Lizzy off to New York with you. You'd better let my parents take care of her if you're not going to act like a mother."

"Act like a mother! Have you looked at your mother lately? Now she's wearing mini skirts, and at her age too!"

"You haven't minded my parents watching Lizzy for the past ten years whenever you wanted to run around," Dad argued.

"I haven't been running around. If we hadn't lived two doors from your parents all these years, she wouldn't be going down there all the time. Good example they are; always taking her to the Legion Hall."

I loved my grandma and grandpa. It made me angry to hear mom talking about them like this. What was wrong with them visiting their friends down at the American Legion Post? Sure, they were there a lot, but unlike my parents, who never did anything together, at least the two of them were hardly ever apart.

I'll admit that Grandma Roy wasn't your average grandma. She wore mini-skirts and high heels, colored her hair red, and played the slot machines and Bingo at the post, but she was fun to be around. I was their only grandchild, so they spoiled me and let me go with them.

"Sure," Mom argued. "Let her grow up thinking all there is to life is Bingo and hanging out with old people.

I say send her to Tennessee to my parents. They'll make sure she grows up right."

I guess she said that because her daddy was a preacher. He and Grandma Puckett lived in Dripping Springs, Tennessee. According to mom, all there was to do there was to go to church and listen to the June bugs hit the screen door. Mom told me that when she was little, she had to go to church three times a week. That didn't sound fun at all. I had never met these grandparents, and the more I thought about it, the more I worried.

"The judge will make the right decision," Grandpa Roy said patting my hand. "After he sees how good we've been taking care of you, there'll be no reason he won't let you stay with us until your parents get this foolish idea of splitting up out of their heads."

"It wouldn't hurt to spruce you up some, Sweetie," Grandma Roy chimed in. "So tomorrow I'm taking you with me to Mary Lou's. You can get your hair done too. Would you like that?"

"Sure, Grandma," I said giving her a little smile. I was looking forward to seeing Grandma's friend, Mary Lou, again. She always kept a big jar of suckers with soft, chewy middles beside her hair dryer. By the time you got down to the chewy part in the middle, the hair on your rollers would be dry.

🍂 🍂 🍂

"Wait until you see Mary Lou's human hair wig now, Lizzy," Grandma said as we drove to Mary Lou's shop the next day. "It's bigger than ever. Why, since the last time you've been to Mary Lou's, I'll bet it's grown six inches taller."

"How did she ever get that thing started?"

"Don't you remember? It was back when Thelma Brooks got cancer and had to have chemotherapy. She was going to lose all her dark black hair, so Mary Lou tried to find her a good wig with real human hair. Only when it came in the mail, it was the wrong color and too thin, so Mary Lou dyed it black. Then when Thelma started losing her hair, she brought it in to Mary Lou so she could blend it in with the hair of the wig to make it look thicker."

"How did she get Thelma's real hair to hold in with the hair of the wig, Grandma?"

"Oh, teasing and lots of hairspray. Lots of hairspray."

"Why does Mary Lou have it now instead of Thelma?"

"When Thelma's real hair began to come back in, she didn't want to be reminded of that terrible time in her life, so she just gave the wig back to Mary Lou."

When we walked in the door of the beauty shop, I could see what Grandma had been talking about. Sitting on a wig stand by the hair dryer was this huge head of hair. It looked like something they would have worn back in the 14th century because it was tall like a cone, but it was also shiny. Layers and layers of hair and hairspray had made it look like it had been shellacked as shiny as a new wooden end table. I was guessing that if I had a tape measure, it would have been two feet around in circumference and two feet tall.

"Hey, if it isn't Lizzy," Mary Lou gushed. "What do you think of it?" she said pointing at the wig.

"It's huge! I'll bet it could be in the *Guinness World Book of Records*."

"That's what I'm hoping for. Now after I cut your grandma's hair, it'll be even bigger."

"But my grandma's hair is red, and your wig is black."

"No problem," Mary Lou laughed. "Here lately, I've just been sticking my customers' hair on there with a little glue and then spray painting it all down with black spray paint at the end of the week. I figured I've already used a case of hairspray on it, so I might as well make it permanent and protect my investment."

"Well, you can add some of Lizzy's hair in today too," Grandma said. "We're sprucing her up for the judge."

"I see." Mary Lou shook her head knowingly. It was obvious that Grandma had told her about my predicament. "How about a shoulder length cut, Lizzy? It would be so cute." Before you knew it I was in the chair and my long hair was coming off.

Grandma had her hair done too, and then we went to the dime store to get a new straw hat for me to wear in the Fourth of July parade on Saturday. Grandma bought a roll of red, white, and blue ribbon in order to decorate it.

"When I get done with this thing," Grandma said as she snipped and twisted ribbons at her kitchen table, "those Auxiliary gals will have to give you the prize for the best hat on the float."

𝆑   𝆑   𝆑

I loved the Fourth of July parade in downtown Indianapolis. The men from the American Legion would wear their uniforms and march in front of the float. The

Ladies' Auxiliary would ride on the float all sporting their homemade decorated hats. Then when we got back to the Legion Hall, there would be a vote for the best hat. Every lady would have a coffee can with her name on it. Men and ladies would place a nickel in the can to vote for their favorite. The proceeds went to the Soldiers' and Sailors' Children's Home in Knightstown, but the woman who was declared the winner got her picture in the Auxiliary newsletter.

That would show the judge, I thought. *If I get my picture in the newsletter, that would prove I was being taken good care of by Grandma and Grandpa Roy.*

ꙮ   ꙮ   ꙮ

The day of the parade was gorgeous. The sun was shining brightly and a blustery breeze was blowing making the American Flags wave to us in the wind like they were happy we were there to take part in the festivities.

"Look, Grandma!" I said as we pulled into the parking lot of the bank where the float was being loaded with Auxiliary ladies. "Mary Lou is wearing that wig as a hat!"

"She sure is and what a display!" Grandma answered excitedly.

Display was mild for it. Mary Lou had flags, ribbons, and silver sticks coming out from that painted and hair-sprayed cone from every direction.

"Wow! Mary Lou," I said running up to her. "That's great! Are those sparklers I see up there?"

"Sure are, Sweetie," she answered. "But don't give away my secret. When we get to the judges' stand, I'm going to

14

light them all up. Won't that be a spectacle? We'll win the float contest for sure."

"I'm sitting by you! I've got to see this! Grandma, come over here. We're going to sit by Mary Lou on the float. Ok?"

Grandma was still making her way onto the float. It was tricky for her to get up on the tongue of the wagon in a mini skirt and two inch heels, but she was pretty spunky. Soon she was seated on the straw bales right next to me and Mary Lou.

"I'd say we're the best looking girls on this float!" Grandma declared. "One of us is going to win the hat contest for sure."

Sandwiched between these two wonderful women, my heart felt warm with contentment. Thoughts of mom and dad's break-up, as Grandma always called it, were as far away as the flag on the top of the Veterans' War Memorial down at the circle.

"Judges' stand to the right!" Mary Lou announced as she pulled her lighter out of her pocket.

"Look!" I shouted. "TV cameras to the left!"

Mary Lou lit the side of the first sparkler she could reach. It was too tall to be lighted from the top. I watched in amazement as the fire took hold and brilliant sparks began to dance on the top of her head. She lit another and another as quickly as she could. I stood up on the bale of straw to get a closer look. Suddenly a ribbon too close to a sparkler caught on fire.

"You're on fire!" I screamed, but Mary Lou could not hear me. The crowd was cheering and Mary Lou was in her glory. She stood up and was waving to the crowd and the judges. All the while, more ribbons and flags were igniting on her head. In a matter of seconds, Mary Lou's wig burst into flames.

I did the only thing I could think of to save her life. I pulled the wig up off of her head so hard that it catapulted into the air like a blazing torch and landed on top of the judges' table where it caught the paper tablecloth and red, white, and blue bunting on fire. A quick-thinking by-stander grabbed the pitcher of lemonade from the table and doused the flames. A quick-thinking TV reporter caught it all on film.

I got my picture in the paper all right, but not for winning the hat contest. Everybody saw me that night on the evening news, including the judge who would decide my custody hearing a month later.

🦅 🦅 🦅

On the day of the hearing, the judge said, "Due to the fact that Lizzy is an only child, and would have access to many cousins and younger relatives to play with in Tennessee, my decision is that the environment there will be more stable and suitable for her. Lizzy Roy will live with Mr. and Mrs. Puckett during the school year. Mr. and Mrs. Roy may have her here in Indianapolis during Christmas and summer vacations. This arrangement will be effective starting September first of this year. This court is adjourned."

🦅 🦅 🦅

"This just isn't going to work!" Grandpa Roy said to his buddies down at the American Legion Post while he,

Grandma, and I were playing Bingo. Actually, I only came along to watch. I wasn't old enough to play the game, but I could help Grandma spot the numbers when they came up. It was pretty hard for her to watch all sixteen cards at once by herself.

"Those Pucketts will fill her mind with all kinds of weird stuff about God and religion," Grandpa said after he'd taken a long drag on his cigarette. He always got wound up when he was sucking smoke through his Lucky Strikes. "You'll see. That judge doesn't know what he's doing. You just wait 'till the rubber hits the road!"

As it turned out, everyone in my family hit the road. Daddy reenlisted in the army, Mom went off to New York to pursue her dreams, and I was put on a train to the great state of Tennessee.

CHAPTER 2

The train ride to Tennessee was the first time I'd ever been away from home.

"You'll love it in Dripping Springs," Mom said as she lifted my small suitcase out of the trunk of her car. We walked without speaking to the platform where I would get on the train. Then as I boarded she said, "There's a waterfall about two miles from Grandma and Grandpa's house. I used to go there sometimes when I wanted to get away from the noise, or when your aunts and uncles were picking on me."

I knew my mom had never fit in with her family in the South. She was the baby and her parents had been very strict. It seemed to her that her siblings always did everything right. She was the rebellious one, always in trouble.

When she was eighteen, she met my daddy at the beach. She'd been invited to go to the ocean with her best friend Susie's family the week after the girls graduated from High School. Susie's family had rented a house on Holden Beach in North Carolina for a whole week. Daddy was on a leave with one of his military buddies. They'd been stationed at Fort Bragg, in Fayetteville, North Carolina, and had taken a three day pass to see the ocean. Now they were on the same stretch of beach as Mom and Susie.

I remembered Mom telling me about it when I was much younger, back in the days when she and my daddy were still friends.

"It was love at first sight," she had said. "For three days on that beach, the four of us were inseparable. Then your daddy asked me for my phone number before he and his friend went back to the base. We wrote to each other every night, and he called me once a week. And of course, my parents had a fit about it! They did everything in the book to convince me not to see him again, but four months later, we ran off and got married without telling anyone but your dad's army buddy and his girlfriend. They were our witnesses at the ceremony."

"Do your mom and daddy know you're married?" I asked.

"Sure they do," she said with a far-off look in her eyes.

"We stopped by Dripping Springs to tell them we were married and moving to Indiana where your daddy was being re-stationed. You'd think they'd have been happy for me. After all, I was eighteen years old, but my mom just stood there and cried. Even my dad cried. I couldn't stand it. I had to get out of there."

That was as much as I could remember ever being told about my Grandma and Grandpa Puckett. Even though mom got a letter from her parents just about once a week, she'd never answered their mail. She and Daddy had never been back to Tennessee in all those years. I had never met my mom's parents. I'd never even seen a picture of them. Now here I was going to live with them.

"Please, Mom," I cried. "Let me go with you."

"Not until I show your daddy I can make something of myself," she answered pulling away from my grasp.

"I'll write to you, baby," Mom said quickly as she left the platform. "Some day you'll see my name in lights. We'll live together in New York City, and while I'm acting, you'll be a fashion model with those long, pretty legs of yours."

Long, pretty legs, I thought those words over as I stared out the train window at the scenery passing by us. That was the first time I could remember her giving me a compliment. A tear plopped down on my lap. I wiped it away from the tanned skin on my legs. I'd worn the shortest shorts a girl could possibly wear in the 60's to get that tan. I wished she would have also told me that I was pretty, but she didn't. Mom had her life to live, her dreams to fulfill of becoming an actress, and those dreams didn't include me. I closed my eyes and tried to picture myself living in her penthouse apartment in New York as the rhythm of the train gently rocked me to sleep.

"Dripping Springs!" the conductor said as he stood next to my seat. "Don't you get off here, Miss?"

"Yes, sir, yes I do," I said quickly pushing myself up in my seat. Suddenly I was terrified of meeting my mother's parents. I grabbed my small cloth covered suitcase and slowly walked toward the back of the train where the conductor was helping people step down to the platform.

"There she is!" a white haired man called out. "I'd know her anywhere. Look at that red hair. She's a carbon copy of our Marjorie."

Is he talking about me? I wondered as two elderly people rushed towards me. He didn't look like a preacher in his bibbed overalls. I had red hair, but my mother's name was Maggie. There must be some other red-haired girl on the platform.

"Helen!" the woman cried, tears streaming down her cheeks. She was smiling and holding out her arms to me.

"This can't be my grandma," I stared in disbelief. She looked like someone out of a nursery rhyme; long dark dress, hair up in a bun, and black stockings barely visible above her black lace up shoes. Before I could protest, the woman hugged me to her ample chest almost taking my breath away.

"We're your Grandma and Grandpa Puckett. We're so glad to have you here with us," she exclaimed suddenly holding me at arms length and looking me over. I took a deep breath and said, "I don't go by Helen. Everyone in Indiana calls me Lizzy."

"Well, how in the world do you get Lizzy out of a beautiful name like Helen?" Grandma Puckett asked with a frown.

"Mom and Daddy named me Helen Louise, but my Grandpa Roy said that name was too stuffy. He started calling me Lizzy, and I guess it stuck."

"Well, for Pete's sake. I've been calling you Helen in my dreams and prayers for the past ten years. How am I going to change now?"

"I think Lizzy is a great name," Grandpa Puckett interrupted. "Once had a milk cow named Lizzy, and she was the best milker I ever had, real friendly too. Don't worry, Mildred. You can do it. All you have to do is practice a little. Come on Lizzy, let's get your bags and load them in the truck."

"This is all I have," I said lifting my small suitcase out at arm's length.

"Mercy, child!" Grandma said. "That thing's not big enough to hold even one dress."

"I don't have any dresses," I said. "I don't need dresses in Indiana. They allow us to wear slacks at school now."

"Well, what do you wear to church?" Grandma asked.

"I don't go to church," I said matter-of-factly. "Mom and Daddy don't go to church either."

Grandma took in a quick breath. "Did you hear that Henry? Our Marjorie doesn't go to church any more."

"Now, Mildred, let's not make a big thing of it in front of Lizzy here. You're going to like church, Lizzy. Surely your mama told you that I'm a preacher, didn't she?"

"You don't look like a preacher. Where's your suit?"

"Oh, I've got one alright. It's a real nice black one. It works for weddings and funerals both. But it doesn't seem to come in too handy when you're milking cows, which is what I had to do before we came to get you this morning."

I looked at Grandpa's big silly grin, and I had to smile thinking about a preacher-man milking cows in his funeral suit. It did seem pretty silly.

"Come on, Helen, I mean Lizzy," Grandma said. "For Pete's sake, child, this is going to take some doing to get your name straight. Let's get on home so I can introduce you to the rest of your kinfolk. They're waiting at our house to meet you."

We walked to the truck and Grandma and Grandpa put me between them on the seat. They were both pretty large people, so I was squished in like a sardine in a can. But later as we curved in and around the mountain, I was glad to have a secure spot so I didn't slide across the seat. You'd have thought I was back in Indianapolis because Grandpa was going around those corners like a driver in the Indy 500.

CHAPTER 3

"Whee!" I screamed. Coming down the other side of the mountain was more fun than going up.

"Slow down, Henry," Grandma pleaded over the roar of the engine. "You're going to scare the girl to death."

"Now, don't get so excited, Mildred. I know what I'm doing, and Lizzy is happy as a lark. Look at her."

I smiled as big as I could at Grandma whose knuckles were white from hanging on to the dashboard.

"This is fun," I assured her. Really! Are we almost there?"

"See that little white square down yonder?" Grandpa said as he pointed down toward a spot in the clearing with his right hand.

"Good gracious!" Grandma screamed. "Keep both of your hands on the wheel, Henry, or we won't make it down to the house alive!"

"Your grandma is what we call, in the preacher business, a worry wart," Grandpa said smiling at Grandma. "She could worry the warts off of a frog. Guess that's why she married me. She needed an old toad around the house."

Grandma just rolled her eyes. "For heaven's sake! I never heard of such dribble."

I laughed at both of them and took a close look at the little white house with a yard out front that seemed to be carved out of the forest surrounding it. It looked like the yard had been salted and peppered. The closer we got to the little farm, the flakes of seasoning began to move and arrange themselves into a line along the lane.

"What in the world is that?" I asked Grandma pointing through the windshield to the scene below. "See those tiny specks all lining up in a row."

"Oh," Grandma answered. "Those aren't specks. Those are your relatives."

Relatives! I thought to myself. *I have that many relatives?*

In a few minutes, we drove into the lane and I got my first peek at the relatives. They were smiling and waving and running behind the car as we proceeded down the lane. By the time we stopped at the little white house, a sea of smiling faces, young and old, surrounded the car.

Grandma opened the door and grabbed my hand. With one pull, I slid across the truck's imitation leather bench seat and plopped out on to the ground feet first like an Olympic gymnast finishing her routine. Grandma pulled me to her side and a mass of people gathered around us holding out their arms trying to get a look at me. I tried to get between Grandma's dress and her soft fleshy arm when Grandpa came to my rescue from the other side of the truck.

"Stand back, now everybody!" Grandpa commanded. "Give her some air. Haven't you ever seen a little red-headed girl before? Bring her over here, Mildred, and we'll introduce her proper-like to everyone."

Grandma pushed me toward Grandpa whose strong arms enveloped me. He turned me around and stood me in front of his bibbed overalls. His big farm hands were on my shoulders as he addressed the crowd.

"This here is our daughter Marjorie's girl, Lizzy Roy. I know you've been praying for her all these years by her given name of Helen Louise, but she's got a nickname of Lizzy. She's pretty used to going by that name so we're going to call her Lizzy too. She's going to stay with us for the school year, so all of you make her feel right at home."

Then the relatives made a big single-file line right in front of Grandma and Grandpa Puckett. One at a time, starting with the older couples, they walked up and introduced themselves. These were Grandma's sisters and brothers and their families. The older ladies had tears in their eyes. They were smiling at Grandma like they had a secret that I knew nothing about. They hugged and kissed me until I was just about worn out.

Next in line were Grandma and Grandpa's children. Each of them told me their names and then the names of my new-found first cousins. There was Uncle Marvin and Aunt Jeanie, Uncle Frank and Aunt Marie, Uncle Leo and Aunt Thelma, and that was just the three oldest boys and their wives. All of their kids were grown and had kids of their own. I looked down the long line for someone the same age as me. Finally I spotted a little girl almost at the end of the line with dark brown hair and freckles smiling at me.

Before long, her mama stepped forward. She was pushing three big boys ahead of her, who seemed reluctant to meet me, and a long string of kids behind her. She had a baby on her hip and a little boy hanging on to her dress.

"Lizzy, I'm your mama's sister, Betty. Actually your mama and I were only one year apart, and even though she was the baby of the family, I was so close to her that I sometimes felt like she was my twin. I miss your mama so much. Oh, listen to me go on." She took a deep breath and started in again.

"Let me introduce you to my whole clan. This here is the baby of the family, Albert. He's two but I can't let him down. He'll take off like a shot. And this little one is Sally." She looked down at the girl clinging to her dress. "She's four and kind of shy, as you can see. Now these big boys here are my oldest: Ted, Ned, and Fred. They're in high school. Next, I had myself three girls: Macy, Stacie, and Lacy. Macy and Stacy are in Junior High School, and Lacy is a sixth grader. And then there's my little Shelby who's the same age as you. You'll be in her fifth grade class in a couple of days."

Shelby gave me a shy little smile and said, "Howdy."

"Now this here is Kim, she's in fourth grade, and Tim is in the third grade. This cutie is Jim. Jim's in the first grade. Well, that's all twelve of them I think. Everybody say 'Hi!' to your cousin, Lizzy."

Aunt Betty squeezed me hard with her free hand and kissed me on the cheek. All the kids were smiling at me and saying, "Hi," but Shelby was grinning from ear to ear. She was wearing a long sleeved blue dress that went almost to her ankles. Suddenly I realized that all the girls were wearing long dresses or skirts. They wore their hair long too. Little girls wore braids and the older women had their hair stuffed up in little hairnets on the backs of their heads. My eyes traveled down to their legs, and to my horror, I saw that they were all wearing black stockings. I looked down at my own tanned legs, and swallowed hard.

"I want to go back to Indiana!" I screamed inside my head where no one could hear me. "What kind of weirdoes are these people?"

CHAPTER 4

"Grandma Puckett," Shelby said with a giggle, "Can I show Lizzy the kittens in the barn?"

"May I show Lizzy?" Grandma corrected her.

"May I?" asked Shelby.

"You may," answered Grandma, "but only for a few minutes. Grandpa will be having a prayer for the meal real soon."

"Ok," Shelby said. "Come with me," she whispered. "I got something real special to show you."

I took Shelby's hand and she led me past all the cousins, and aunts, and uncles, and tables with red checkered tablecloths loaded with foods of every kind, until we turned the corner of the house and I saw the biggest red barn I'd ever seen in my life.

Actually it kind of looked like the ones in the magazine ads for chewing tobacco, but without the words on the side.

We ran to the door, and suddenly my heart started thumping. It was dark in the barn, even though the sun was shining brightly outside. It smelled musty and sweet and stinky all at the same time. There were noises from animals I couldn't identify in the dark, and I wasn't sure where to step.

"I don't think I want to go in," I said pulling my hand out of Shelby's.

"Why not? It's just a barn."

"I've never been in a barn before," I told her hoping she wouldn't laugh.

"That's ok." Shelby put her arm around me. "I don't reckon there are many barns in Indianapolis. Come on," she said gently leading me forward. "There's nothing in here that can hurt you. There's Grandpa's milk cow, Fern, but she's tied up to that railing over there. And there's Grandpa's old mule, Stubborn. He won't get out of his stall. That'd be too much work. And there's Mama Cat, the one who's got the new babies. Come on. I'll show you where she's hid 'em."

I cautiously followed Shelby looking back to see if the cow and mule were following us, but they weren't. My eyes were adjusting to the darkness as I picked my way to the corner. Shelby took me to a pile of hay bales stacked three high on top of each other. There was a big space between two of the bales on the top layer like someone had pulled a bale off after they'd been stacked. Shelby and I climbed up to where the space was and saw five little black kittens sleeping on top of each other in a pile.

"You wanna hold one?" Shelby picked up a little black ball of fur with a pink nose and held it out to me.

"Yes, please!" I sat down on the bale and Shelby passed the kitten to me. It was soft and wiggly. It tried to pull itself up on my shirt, but then fell back down in my lap, meowing until I picked it up and held it against my chest. All of my life I had wanted to have a kitten to love, but Mom and Daddy would never allow it.

"We can't have cats in this apartment," Daddy had said. "So just get the idea out of your mind, Lizzy."

"And even if we could," Mom continued, "You'd only get attached to it, and then it would up and die on you."

I guess she never realized I was dying of loneliness. Sure, I had Grandma and Grandpa Roy, and all of their friends at the Legion during the day, but at night I was all by myself. I had friends at school, but I never asked them over. If Mom and Daddy were fighting, as they often were, I would scrunch under my covers and cry myself to sleep.

"Can I keep it?" I asked Shelby who had picked up another one of the kittens.

"Why would you want to do that? They're just barn cats. Grandma won't allow them in the house. Why, Daisy would have a fit!"

"Who's Daisy?"

"Daisy is Grandma's dumb old poodle; the one Grandpa got her after your mama runned away with the soldier man."

"Hey! That's my daddy you're talking about!" Tears stung at my eyes, and I laid the kitten back down on the pile and looked down at my knees.

"Oh, Lizzy, I'm so sorry. I didn't mean to hurt you. Please forgive me," Shelby pleaded. "If Grandma knew I talked about your mama and daddy and hurt your feelings, she'd get after me with the wooden spoon."

I looked at Shelby's little face. She looked so pitiful that I broke out laughing and Shelby gave me a frown.

"I'm sorry I laughed, but you ought to see your face, Shelby. Does she really hit you with a wooden spoon?"

"Well, not exactly. You see, one time I kicked that old poodle, and Grandma got after me with the wooden spoon. Only I can run faster than her and I runned all the way home. Bad part was that when I got there, she'd done called my mama on the phone, so I got a whipping anyhow. Please say you forgive me, Lizzy."

"Sure, I forgive you, Shelby. What did you mean when you said Grandpa got it for her after my mom ran away?"

"Well, from what my aunts and uncles said, Grandma just about went crazy after your mama married your daddy. She was so depressed that she just sat in her rocker saying, 'My baby. My baby.' Grandpa tried everything he could to get her to snap out of it, but it just wasn't working.

Then one day somebody left an old miniature poodle on the church steps that was about to die. Grandpa brought her home even though he knew our grandma didn't allow no pets in the house. At first Grandma was mad as an old wet hen, but then she felt so sorry for the old thing that she cleaned it up and started nursing it back to health. Grandpa says that God must have sent that old dog, because she done worked a miracle on Grandma."

"So does everyone in the family hate my mother?"

"No, Lizzy," Shelby said taking my hand. "We all love your mama and you too. Why the grownups are always talking about you in their prayers. Ever since I can remember, my family has been praying for your family. I guess we just don't know why your parents ain't spoken to Grandma and Grandpa all these long years. I guess that's why some folks might think they run out on all of us. But we're not mad at you, I promise."

"Well, I'm mad at them," I said with tears filling my eyes. "They ran out on me too! I can't help it. I hate them, but I still love them. Do you know what I mean, Shelby?"

"Yeah, I know. I hate that old poodle, because she nips at me sometimes, but I love her because she helped Grandma feel better. Still, I sure don't like it when Grandma takes the wooden spoon out of the drawer."

Just then, we heard the big dinner bell clanging from the direction of the house.

"We'd better get going," Shelby said, "or we might both get a feel of that wooden spoon."

We jumped down from the straw bales and took off like a shot out of a cannon. I wasn't going to get a spanking on my first day in Tennessee!

CHAPTER 5

"Now everybody gather round," Grandpa Puckett announced, "and I'm going to ask the blessing on this food. But I know that the Good Lord's already blessed it because my nose is telling my heart that you fine ladies outdid yourselves today!"

Everybody smiled and put their chins down on their chests and closed their eyes. I looked at Shelby and she had her head down too, so I lowered my chin, but I took a peek at the people crowding around Grandpa Puckett as he spoke. Each face had a little smile and every once in a while someone would say, "Amen" or "Thank you, Jesus." Then I heard Grandpa say my name and I looked right up at his down turned face.

"And dear Lord, please let our little Lizzy feel right at home here in our big family. And Lord, thank you so much for answering our prayers after all these long hard years, when we never knew what was happening to her as she was growing up. Thank you, Lord, for keeping her safe. In Jesus' name, Amen."

I watched a little tear fall from Grandpa's chin as "Amens" erupted from the faces all around me. And when the people opened their eyes, they were all looking at me smiling and winking and patting me on the back. They pushed me toward the long tables loaded with food. I grabbed Shelby's hand and drug her along with me. I'd never been first in line for a food table in Indianapolis. There was always an American Legion Commander and his wife who would be asked to go first. Grandma and Grandpa Roy would always be talking to their friends, and we'd end up at the end of the line scraping the crusty parts off the casserole dishes.

Shelby and I grabbed a plate and started down the tables from both sides. I had never seen so much food in my life. There was fried chicken, baked ham, roasted turkey, ham loaf, and meatloaf. There were beans of every kind. Some were green, some were baked, some were pickled, and some were deep inside steaming casseroles with crumbled onions on the top. There was corn on the cob, corn off the cob, and corn fixed in ways I'd never seen before. There were lettuce salads, gelatin salads, and fruit salads. There were breads and muffins of every kind and flavor. There was watermelon, muskmelon, and honeydew melon. There were cakes and cookies by the dozen, and even homemade ice cream with strawberries. It was a good thing my shorts had an elastic waist band. Shelby and I tested every one of the cookies, and there wasn't one of them that we didn't like.

After we ate, the men played horseshoes and the women cleaned up the mess. Then they sat in rockers on the porch and talked as the rhythm of their rockers blended with their voices into a kind of music all its own, speeding up when they were in hot debate and slowing down when they agreed on a particular topic. Shelby and I played with all the smaller cousins until we were out of breath from laughing and running around the house. All too soon it was dark, and Grandpa and Grandma Puckett were kissing their grandchildren goodbye. Shelby had to go home with her family, but Grandma promised I'd get to see her the very next day at church.

"You'll be in my Sunday school class," Shelby whispered. And I stood there wondering, *What is a Sunday school class?*

"Come on, dear," Grandma said. "Let's see about putting you to bed."

We walked by Daisy who was stretched out on a rug by the back door.

"I didn't see your dog outside all day today, Grandma."

"Oh, there was too much commotion out there for her today. She stays inside if there are lots of people around. She's getting old, just like me," Grandma groaned as she climbed the steps. "Just don't tease her and the two of you will get along just fine. Do you like dogs, Helen?"

"It's Lizzy, Grandma."

"Of course it is, and I'll catch on to it presently. Just be patient with your old Grandma, child." She turned on a little dresser lamp and waved her hand around the room. "Now this is going to be your room, Honey. It used to be your mama's room when she was your age. I've got you a nice new nightgown laid out here on the bed. You go ahead and get into it, and I'll take your dirty clothes downstairs with me."

I slipped into the nightgown, and then before Grandma could go out the door, I grabbed her long dress.

"Grandma, where's the bathroom? I have to go."

"Oh, Honey, I'm sorry. I forgot you don't know your way around here. Just a minute and I'll get it for you."

Get it for me, I wondered. *What does she mean by that?* Just then Grandma reached under the bed and pulled out a little white porcelain pot. She sat it next to the dresser and took the lid off.

"Here you go, Honey. Just put the lid back on when you're done and I'll throw it out in the morning." With that, she turned and walked out the door as I stared at the pot with my mouth wide open.

CHAPTER 6

I woke up to birds chirping outside my window. I sat up and saw birds of every color. There were blue ones, red ones, and yellow ones sitting in the tree right outside my bedroom. The blue bird and the yellow bird started chasing each other and the red bird was singing a sweet little song. *Even the birds here are friendly,* I thought. The only birds I saw outside my window in Indiana were starlings and pigeons.

A smell of frying bacon was wafting up the stairs into my bedroom. Breakfast! I thought, and it's something hot!

I slipped out of my bed and went over to the big wooden dresser at the far side of the room. I opened the first drawer and was surprised to see plain white cotton underwear. It didn't look like mine, because mine had the days of the week printed up near the waistband. There were other things in the drawer that I didn't recognize. Some looked like little white sleeveless dresses. Some looked like grown up stockings, except they were black instead of tan like mom's, and they were thick like dancer's tights.

I wonder if these were my mom's clothes and Grandma just never got rid of them, I thought as I sorted through the underclothes.

Then I opened the next drawer expecting to find my shorts and tops. But this drawer only held my hairbrush, toothbrush and toothpaste The last drawer was empty.

Where is my suitcase? I wondered as I searched around the room. I got down on my knees and looked under the bed. *There it is!*

I was relieved since I thought I'd lost my clothing and other possessions like my little red, white, and blue purse Grandma Roy gave me last Independence Day, and my pink foam curlers for when I wanted my shoulder length hair to have some bounce. But when I opened the suitcase, it was empty! Completely empty!

I was just getting ready to yell for Grandma when she started coming up the stairs making each one creak and groan as she slowly put one foot in front of the other. When she got to the top, she peeked in my doorway and said, "Morning. How would you like some bacon and eggs for breakfast?"

"I'd like my clothes, Grandma," I said. "What did you do with them and my other things? My suitcase is empty."

"Well, it's like this, Helen."

"It's Lizzy, Grandma."

"Yes, well, it's like this Lizzy," Grandma fumbled with the pocket on her apron.

"You won't need any of those fancy play clothes while you are here. We don't wear things like that up here in the hills. Why, the bugs would eat you alive in those short pants, so I've put them away for a little while until you go home in the spring."

"Well, what am I going to wear, Grandma? I can't go out in my nightgown."

"No you certainly can't," Grandma said with a chuckle. "From the moment I knew you were coming, I started sewing you a whole new wardrobe. Just look and see."

She opened the closet and I saw a whole bunch of dresses hanging from the rod. Some were pretty flowered patterns and some were plain blue or green. All of them had long sleeves and looked like they would go down to my ankles. Down on the floor was a pair of black tie-up shoes like I'd seen Shelby wearing yesterday.

"Grandma, do I have to wear these long sleeved dresses in the summertime?"

"Of course, honey. Everybody in our church wears these kinds of dresses. You'll see. They're really comfortable and they cover your body so you're modest and proper. Now let's pick one out for church this morning."

This is crazy, I thought as Grandma held a light green dress up to my chin.

"Oh, Lizzy, this looks ever so pretty with your red hair. Try this one on for your grandma. Oh, I almost forgot. I didn't show you your new slips and stockings."

At that she went to the dresser and pulled a white cotton slip out of the drawer and a black pair of stockings. Then she laid them on the bed, and stood smiling down at me like I should know what to do next. A little tear started forming on the rim of my bottom eyelid. I blinked several times determined not to let it trickle down my face.

"Are you two girls coming down to eat any time soon?" Grandpa Puckett yelled up the stairway.

"We'll be right down, Henry," Grandma yelled back.

"Now, Lizzy, be a sweetheart and put your clothes on. Grandpa has to eat plenty early on Sundays or he might just burp during the sermon, and that wouldn't do at all." Grandma pushed me toward the clothing lying on the bed.

"I'll get your grandpa's breakfast on the table, and you come down as soon as you can." Then she creaked back down the stairs and left me looking at a pile of stuff I had no idea how to put on by myself.

CHAPTER 7

Grandma had to help me get my clothes on after I didn't come down for breakfast.

"I declare," she said as she finished buttoning the back of my dress. "I forgot you aren't used to dressing up there in Indiana. I thought that my daughter had been taking you to church, and you'd know how to put on a slip and stockings by yourself since you've already turned ten years old. But don't you worry your pretty little red head about it. I'm going to make sure you learn everything a girl your age has to know by the time you go back up north."

"What would that be, Grandma?" I asked arching my back as she tied the big sash around my middle into a bow the size of a dinner plate.

"Why just everything," she said with a smile, "like cooking, cleaning, gardening, sewing, knitting, and of course, proper manners for a young lady. And lesson number one in proper manners is to not keep your grandpa waiting in the morning or his breakfast will get cold."

She turned me around and gave me a little push toward the stairway. I had to be careful to hold on to the banister because the long dress made it hard for me to see my feet.

As soon as we finished eating, Grandma, Grandpa, and I got into the truck and headed to church. We followed the little mountain path we'd been on before except that this time it curved around in the valley making twists and turns that could make your breakfast want to come back up. Occasionally we'd get close to the side of the mountain. It was always outside Grandma's window and at times looked close enough to reach out and touch.

"Why is water running down the side of the rock, Grandma? It didn't rain last night."

"You're right, Honey. It didn't rain down here, but it rained somewhere up there. Now that water is running all the way down here to keep this entire valley green and growing. There are springs in the hills that spill over and in some places they make the prettiest waterfalls a body can ever hope to see. When we go around this little bend, you're going see one that everybody round here has taken a liking to."

Maybe this is the falls that Mom told me about, I thought as I strained to look up the rock wall out of the windshield.

"There's a little bridge we're going to go over and then you'll see it," Grandma said excitedly.

We turned toward the curve of the mountain and I saw a little wooden bridge right ahead. I looked up toward the rock wall outside Grandma's window and saw a beautiful cascade of water that looked like it started from a tiny hole up near the tree tops and landed in a pool at the base of the mountain forming the little river that ran under the bridge.

"Ooh! It's beautiful!" I whispered. "Does it have a name, Grandma?"

"Well, from watching most of the young folk and tourists that come through here you'd think it was called Wishing Falls," she said. "People stand here on the bridge and make wishes as they throw their pennies into the pool. But your grandpa and I don't hold to making wishes like that. We call it by its real name, Promise Falls, like the old timers here on the mountain have called it since this part of Tennessee was settled."

"Why did they call it Promise Falls? Did they stand on the bridge and make a promise?"

"No, Lizzy," Grandpa answered.

"They called it Promise Falls because sometimes when the sun is just right, a rainbow appears in the treetops hovering over the falls. Some of the first settlers struggled so hard to get over these mountains, and when they came to this falls and saw the flat land below in the valley, and the rainbow at the top of the falls, it was like God was talking to them himself, telling them that he had just brought them into the Promised Land. It's a good land where your kinfolk grew up, worshiped the Lord, lived, died, and were buried. I guess it is kind of like the Promised Land to your grandma and me too. And the first thing those settlers did was build a church by this falls so they could thank the good Lord for all he'd done for them."

As if on cue, we pulled into the church parking lot where a hand carved wooden sign proclaimed, "Promise Falls Church of God." The little white church was nestled in a backdrop of trees with the mountains towering behind them, but the front yard was flat and grass covered. Grandpa stopped the truck and breathed in the morning air until his chest touched the steering wheel.

"Thirty-nine years I've been pulling in here on Sunday mornings, Lizzy, and each time it feels like my first Sunday. I breathe in God's goodness and thank him for letting me serve him here in this place. Pretty soon, I'm hoping you'll feel as much at home here as I do."

That is going to be a miracle, I thought to myself looking back and forth between the two of them, smiles lighting up their faces, *because going to church is as foreign to me as going to the moon.*

CHAPTER 8

Grandpa Puckett had only been preaching for ten minutes, but it seemed like ten hours. I grabbed for the fan in the back of the pew that advertised Hutchinson Funeral Home and fanned myself furiously, but every inch of my body felt hot and itchy. The cotton slip had some kind of lace around the neck, sleeves, and hem line that constantly poked me, and the stockings were heavy and hot. My feet were crying to be free from the lace up shoes, and I really had to go to the bathroom. I didn't dare ask Grandma about that during the service. She might just pull a porcelain pot out from under the pew like she had from under my bed the night before. No, I'd better just do my best to hold it and not fidget too much. I decided that as soon as the service ended, I could run out behind some of those trees if I had to.

The only thing that made me happy was seeing Shelby two rows behind me. Every once in a while I would turn around and give her a smile. Once she waved back at me with her funeral fan and mouthed, "You look pretty." That made me grin even more until Grandma put her hand on my knee and gave me a look that said, "Turn around and pay attention."

The longer Grandpa preached, the louder he got. And the louder he got, the redder his face became. I didn't understand what the fuss was all about. He used words I didn't understand like justification and sanctification. The only "cation" word I knew was vacation and this service was none of the sort.

Just about the time I thought Grandpa was going to burst, he suddenly got really quiet and picked up his hymnal. All of the grownups turned to the right page and started singing. They sang and sang while Grandpa begged the people to come down to the front and give their hearts to Jesus.

I wasn't sure who Jesus really was. I'd heard his name before, but only when someone in my family was really mad. Then they used his middle name too, like when Mom is really mad at me and calls me Helen Louise. Then that got me to thinking that if Jesus was his first name and Christ was his middle name, then what was his last name? Maybe they would tell me that in the class that was supposed to come after the morning service; the Sunday school. Then I would get to talk to Shelby again, but only after I found a tree out back first.

After grandpa said the final prayer, I squeezed past grandma and ran for the door. Shelby was right behind me. She caught me half-way to the tree line.

"Where are you going, Lizzy?" she yelled as she caught my arm. "You running away from church?"

"No," I said, "I'm running for the trees. If I don't, I'm going to wet my pants and stockings and everything else."

"Why don't you use the outhouse?" she said pointing to a little building to my right.

"What's an outhouse?" I asked jumping from one foot to the other.

"It's where proper ladies use the bathroom, not behind a tree."

She took my hand and pulled me toward the little building. Once I understood what she was talking about, I ran for the door and made it just in time.

"Do Grandma and Grandpa have one of these?" I asked when I emerged from the little building.

"Sure, it's out east of the barn. We went right by it when we went to look at the kittens last night."

"That makes me feel a lot better," I said relieved to have gotten over the first big hurdle of living with my grandparents; knowing where to use the bathroom. Everything else would work itself out too, I was sure.

Shelby led me back into the church and down into the basement. There we went into a little room with three other kids. The teacher was Mrs. Harley. She smiled at me and asked Shelby to introduce her friend to the class.

"This is my first cousin, Lizzy, all the way from Indiana to spend the school year with Grandma and Grandpa Puckett," Shelby said proudly.

I smiled at the three dark-headed boys who were staring at me like I had two heads. Two of them looked like twins, and they were about our age. Shelby told me later that they were just brothers. Sammy Ray was a sixth grader, and his brother, Jimmy Ray, was in our class. The other boy, Jacob, was a sixth grader too and he was Mrs. Harley's son. He was looking me up and down with a frown on his face.

"Well, welcome to our intermediate class, Lizzy," Mrs. Harley said beaming. "You're the little girl we've been praying about for ever so long. Come take a seat and we'll start today's lesson."

That last remark puzzled me. What did she mean that I was the little girl they'd been praying for? How could they pray about me when they didn't even know me? As the hour went on, I had more questions in my mind than hairs on my head.

Mrs. Harley was talking about a man named Abraham who had a baby when he was a hundred years old. His wife was close to 90. Mrs. Harley said Abraham trusted God, and so God kept his promise to give Abraham and Sarah a son.

My daddy wasn't even 30 and he couldn't stand having a kid around, I thought. *How could a 90 year old woman have enough energy to run after a baby? And how could a 100 year old man teach his son to play ball? This stuff is so confusing. I'll have to ask Grandpa about it after class. After all, he is the preacher. He should be able to explain it to me.*

When a bell rang, Mrs. Harley dismissed us from Sunday school and Shelby and I headed out the door. Jacob came up behind us and said, "Well if it isn't little Miss Bluebird who can't read a word." Then he yanked on Shelby's bow at the back of her dress until it came untied and ran off out of the basement.

"What's that all about?" I asked Shelby as she retied her dress.

"Oh, Jacob Harley makes me so mad I could just spit, but his mom's my Sunday school teacher, so I can't say anything about how he treats me to anybody. They'd all just tell me to get along with him," she sighed.

"Why did he call you Miss Bluebird?"

"Well, see, when I was in second grade, Mrs. Frost put us in reading groups. I was in the bluebirds, and Jimmy

Ray was in the Cardinals. Everybody knew the Cardinals were the good readers and the bluebirds were the dummies. Jimmy told Jacob I was in the bluebirds and he's teased me ever since. I got better at reading in the third grade, but I just have such a hard time with some of those words. Sometimes I can't make any sense out of them. Mama says I'm just a slow starter and I'll catch on to it soon enough."

"And I'm going to help you," I promised, feeling guilty since I was in the top reading group in my last school. I wondered if I'd ever made the slow readers in my class feel as bad as Jacob had done to Shelby.

"That Jacob Harley is going to wish he never met Lizzy Roy." I took Shelby's hand as we went up the basement steps. Grandma met us at the top.

"I've been looking for you two girls. Come on now. We've been invited over to your house for lunch, Shelby."

"Yippee!" yelled Shelby. "Come on, Lizzy. You can ride with us."

CHAPTER 9

"How am I going to fit in there?" I stared in disbelief at Shelby's parents' station wagon.

"It's easy! Ted, Ned, and Fred always sit in the last seat that faces backward. Before papa shuts the tailgate, we'll sit on their laps."

I looked into the car. The three oldest boys were already sitting in the back seat with Shelby's little brother, Tim, on one of the boy's laps. There were six kids in the middle seat; four bigger kids on the seat and two younger kids on their laps. Aunt Betty was in the passenger side front seat with one arm wrapped tightly around little Albert's waist sitting beside her. Uncle Don was coming around to the back of the car to shut the tailgate. Quickly, Shelby and I jumped up into the rear of the station wagon before Uncle Don locked us in.

I was sitting on Ted's lap. He was the oldest; ready to start his senior year in High School. Shelby was beside me on Ned's lap. She reintroduced me to everyone and they tried to make small talk, but I felt like the world was closing in on me. Even though Uncle Don had left the back window down a little, I could hardly breathe.

"How do you ride like this every Sunday to church?" I asked Shelby.

"You get used to it. But we don't just go to church on Sunday mornings. There's Sunday night service too, and Wednesday night Bible study. And in the fall, we'll have revival. That'll last two weeks. It's a lot of fun."

I must have groaned, because Shelby said, "You alright, Lizzy?"

"Yes, I'm alright." But in my mind I was thinking, *Maybe if I write to Grandpa Roy, he'll come right down here and get me.* It was going to take a lot of doing to make going to church that often seem like fun.

Just when I thought I couldn't stand being cooped up in that station wagon any longer, we pulled into Uncle Don and Aunt Betty's lane. They lived in a much bigger house than Grandma and Grandpa Puckett. It was two stories tall and seemed to go on forever. A big barn stood out behind it and fences kept all of the farm animals from getting out into the wide front yard. Grandma and Grandpa Puckett's truck pulled right in behind us.

"Now you kids get washed up while Stacy and Lacy set the table," Aunt Betty said as she ushered us all into the house. Shelby and I went to the kitchen sink and washed our hands.

"Come see my room," Shelby said as she grabbed my hand and pulled me up the stairs. There were three bedrooms upstairs. One was shared by the three oldest boys. A big double bed was on one wall and a twin bed on the opposite wall. A small three drawer dresser sat in the corner. The bedroom next to this one was shared by the younger boys. Albert was still in a baby bed. Jim and Tim shared a double bed. The last room was for all six of the girls.

"This here is my room," Shelby said shyly. Ain't it just grand?" There was a double bed on one wall and a bunk bed that was four beds high on the other wall.

"Wow! I've never seen a bunk bed that high! Who sleeps on the top?"

"I do! Mama moved me up there just this year. Daddy put that rail up there for me so I wouldn't fall out. Come on up. I'll show you."

A ladder had been fixed into the end of the beds so that it was part of the bunks and couldn't come off. I climbed and climbed until I got up to Shelby's bed. She was right behind me urging me on.

"Now, lower your head and crawl onto the mattress. Keep on going so I can fit up there with you."

If I felt claustrophobic in the car, I really felt breathless now. Shelby and I couldn't even sit up. We had to lie on our sides facing each other to talk, and there was no way I was going to lay on the open side with the railing. I made sure my back was to the wall.

"Isn't it grand up here?" Shelby giggled.

"Aren't you afraid to sleep up here Shelby? What if you have to go to the bathroom in the night? How would you ever get down by yourself in the dark?"

"Shucks, I never have to go to the bathroom in the night. That's why Mama said I could be on the top. I never have an accident, and I hardly ever get sick to my stomach like Sally does. That's why Sally has to sleep on the bottom bunk, because she sometimes gets a stomach ache and mama has to have her on ground level."

"Where did you ever find a bed like this?"

"Daddy done made it for us. My daddy's a wood-worker you know, and he can make beautiful furniture. Wait 'til you see our kitchen table."

"Shelby! Lizzy! Lunch is ready," Aunt Betty called up the stairwell.

Shelby showed me how to back my way down the bunk bed ladder, and we hurried to the kitchen.

Uncle Don had done some marvelous work in there. The room was huge. It was not only the kitchen, but the dining room besides. There was a handsome oak hutch on the wall between the part where the cooking was done and the part where everyone ate. The table was bigger than anything I'd seen in my life. There were only four big chairs and a highchair at one end of the table. These were for the adults and baby Albert. Everyone else sat at long benches all the way around the rest of the table. After everyone was seated, Uncle Don, who was sitting at the head of the table, said a prayer. When he was finished, everybody said, "Amen!"

Uncle Don had a pile of 17 empty plates stacked up in front of him, and Aunt Betty had placed the platters of food at that end too. Uncle Don began to dish up a plate for each person starting with the kids on the bench at the other end of the table. He filled the first plate and then passed it to Grandma, who passed it to Macy, who passed it to Stacie, who passed it to Lacy, who passed it to Kim, who passed it to Shelby, who passed it to me. I was sitting next to Tim, so I gave it to him. Suddenly another plate appeared and I passed it down. Another came after that, and I passed it down.

After I'd passed several plates, Shelby whispered, "You keep this one, Lizzy. Look, Daddy gave you a drumstick 'cause you're company. I wish I'd get a drumstick some-time. I usually get the wing or the back."

Shelby got her plate next and sure enough, she had a chicken wing on it. We also had mashed potatoes and gravy, green beans, sliced tomatoes and a thick chunk of bread on our plates. I was so amazed at the passing of plates that I watched them going until everyone had one in front of them. Just about the time I picked up my chicken leg, a plate came from my right.

"Give this to Daddy," Tim said. "Jim wants some more mashed potatoes and gravy." I passed the plate on to Shelby, who passed it up the line to be refilled. Then Tim tapped me on the shoulder again.

"Lizzy, please pass this to Daddy. Ned wants some more green beans." I passed the plate to Shelby and she handed me Jim's refilled plate to pass on to Tim.

"When do I eat?" I whispered to Shelby when she passed me Ned's refilled plate on its way down the table. "All I've done is pass plates." Then Shelby burst out giggling and almost fell off of her bench.

"What's going on, girls?" Aunt Betty asked. When Shelby repeated the whole story, everyone laughed and Uncle Don said, "No more seconds on that side of the table, boys, until Lizzy gets something to eat."

When I rode home with Grandma and Grandpa later that afternoon, I no longer felt squished between them. I felt I was riding in a limousine.

CHAPTER 10

Shelby was right, we no sooner got home from our afternoon at her house, and Grandpa told Grandma that she and I had better get cleaned up for Sunday evening services. He had to go over to the church early because he'd left his sermon notes on the pulpit. So once again, we hopped in the truck and headed back to Promise Falls Church of God. This time I knew where to look for the falls and sure enough, there was a rainbow up at the top.

"Look, Grandpa. I see the rainbow!"

"Yes sir-ee! That's a dandy!"

"Do you think God is making a promise to me like he did to that Abraham guy we learned about this morning?" I asked. "Of course, I don't mean that I want to have a baby at 100 years old or anything like that, but do you think he knows I'm down here and he's saying, 'I promise you, Lizzy, everything will turn out all right?'"

"Honey, he knows you're down here all right. He put you right here with Grandma and me on purpose just so you can be loved and get to know him better. Ain't that so, Mildred?"

Grandma just shook her head yes and blotted her eyes with a hankie pulled from the sleeve of her dress.

We pulled into the church lot and Grandma said, "Come on in the church, Honey, and I'll get you some crayons from the Sunday school room. You could draw a picture of that rainbow you saw."

We went down to Mrs. Harley's room and found some crayons and paper in the cabinet.

"You go ahead and draw, Lizzy. I'm going to go practice the organ, and I'll come down and get you when the people start coming in for evening services."

"I didn't know you played the organ, Grandma. You didn't play this morning."

"Well, I'm trying to let some of the younger women take a whack at it. I started playing when I wasn't much older than you. After fifty years of pounding on that pump organ, it just about tuckers me out to do a whole morning service. We'll only sing a few hymns tonight, and that's more my speed."

I could hear Grandma playing the organ as I colored my rainbow. I was just putting the finishing touches on my waterfall when I heard someone walking in the basement. I looked up expecting to see Grandma, but instead it was Jacob Harley.

"Hey, what are you doing down here?" he demanded. "This is my mom's classroom and those are her crayons and paper you're using up."

"Well, my Grandpa owns this church and his best friend is God, so I guess my two kings beats your one queen, Buster." I'd learned poker from Grandpa Roy, and this kid sounded like some of the hard headed friends Grandpa played cards with. I wasn't sure Grandpa owned the church, but sometimes a bluff will make the other guy lay down his cards and even get up from the table.

"Whoa now, Red! I always heard that redheads had a hot temper. Now I know it's true. You just startled me being here in my mom's room is all. She sent me down here to get her lesson book. You don't need to get all huffy."

"Seems to me that you're the one that got huffy."

Just then Shelby stuck her head in the doorway.

"Lizzy, Grandma told me to come down here and get you," she said shyly looking at Jacob like he was the big bad wolf.

"I'm coming." I quickly put the crayons back in the cabinet.

Then Jacob turned to Shelby. "Is she going to sit by you so she can read the words out of the hymnal to you, Miss Bluebird?"

"Come on Shelby," I said grabbing her hand. "Best leave the rats in the basement where they belong."

We headed up the steps, but not fast enough for Shelby not to hear Jacob's parting words. "Just wait until we get to school tomorrow."

CHAPTER 11

I had to get dressed quickly the next morning because I was going to ride the bus! In Indianapolis, I could walk from my house to my school, and Grandma and Grandpa Roy's house was just down the street from mine. Riding the bus would be on the top of my list of great adventures for this day. The second thing would be eating a lunch that I didn't fix myself. I had always packed my own lunches because mom would sleep in. It was her beauty sleep she said, but sometimes it was because she had a hangover. Sometimes there was bologna in the house, but most days I was stuck with peanut butter and jelly. Grandma had told me she was going to be packing my lunch, and I was anxious to get downstairs to see what it would be.

"Are we poor, Grandma?" I asked looking at the paper sack on the counter.

"Heavens no, child," Grandma said wrapping a fried chicken leg in waxed paper. "We don't have a lot of money, but we're rich in everything that really counts. Why do you ask?"

"Well, in Indianapolis, I had a red lunchbox and the poor kids had brown paper sacks."

"You don't need to worry about that here. Most everybody will be having a brown paper sack. Besides, it isn't what's on the outside that counts, when there's chicken, carrot strips, and Snicker doodles on the inside."

"Yummy!" I said remembering the cookies from the day before at Shelby's house. I knew Aunt Betty had sent a box full of stuff home with Grandma after lunch.

"And don't be forgetting what you and I talked about on the way home from church, Lizzy," Grandpa said from his spot at the kitchen table. "People are the same way. You can't judge a book by its cover. You're going meet a lot of new people today. Give them all a chance before you go making your opinions of them."

"Ok, Grandpa," I said remembering the talk on the ride home. I'd told Grandpa that I was nervous to start school and meet all the new kids the next day. I didn't tell him of Jacob's threat, but I did ask why Mrs. Harley was so nice and her son was so mean.

"Well, that's got lots of people baffled," Grandpa had said, "but in God's timing, we're all praying he'll come around and his daddy too." No further explanation was given, and I didn't get a chance to ask, because Grandpa started singing a hymn at the top of his voice. Then Grandma joined in, and pretty soon, I found myself singing along even though I didn't know many of the verses.

It was something about an amazing girl named Grace. I guess she had saved this guy from a terrible life. He felt so bad about himself that he called himself a wrench. Well, if this girl, Grace, could save that guy, maybe a hack saw like Jacob Harley could somehow be helped, but I didn't know who would be able to do it. I hoped it wouldn't have to be me.

"Here comes the bus!" Grandma said excitedly while she handed me my paper sack, a box of new crayons, a scissors, a notepad, and two new sharpened pencils. She pushed me toward the lane.

"Have a good day today, Helen. I'll be praying for you back here at home."

I ran down to the end of the lane, my heart beating fast. I was surprised to see Uncle Don was the driver.

"Morning, Lizzy," he said smiling. "Just go take a seat." A sudden relief flooded over me as I walked down the aisle. The bus looked almost full, because ten of Uncle Don's kids were already seated. I already knew half the kids who would be riding the bus! I saw Shelby right away sitting a few rows from the front, and I sat down with her.

"Do you know who our teacher will be?"

"Sure, it'll be Mrs. Higgins. She's been teaching fifth grade for years. Even Daddy had her for his fifth grade teacher."

"Is she nice?"

"She's pretty strict, my brothers and sisters say, but Daddy says to give her a chance to like me before I make my mind up about her."

"Sounds like the advice Grandpa gave me last night when I asked him why Jacob Harley was so mean. Does he ride this bus?"

"No, he don't."

"Good, maybe we won't even run into him today since he's in the sixth grade," I offered optimistically.

"I wish that was the case," Shelby sighed, "but fifth and sixth grade eat lunch and go to recess at the same time. We'll see him alright. I just hope he don't see us."

❧ ❧ ❧

Uncle Don's last stop of the morning was at a cabin in a wooded lot that looked like it was about to fall down. There was an old wringer washer on the front porch along with a rocker and two huge hound dogs. A high school girl with tons of make-up, teased up hair, penny loafer shoes, and a tight sweater with a big BB stitched on it, came out of the house. When she got on the bus, she smiled at all of the big boys as she went past them and stuck her nose up at the girls. Then she grabbed a little kid by the arm and said, "Go sit somewhere else, Kenny." She took his seat so she could sit behind two smiling big boys who looked like they couldn't get their eyes off of her sweater.

"Who's that?" I asked Shelby.

"That's Brenda Bower, and you don't want to get any-where near her," Shelby whispered. "She's got long painted fingernails that can scratch you really bad if you're sitting in the seat she wants."

"She doesn't scare me," I said bravely, but secretly I hoped to stay away from the bully with the BB on her chest.

CHAPTER 12

"Shelby Puckett," Mrs. Higgins called out.

"Here, ma'am," Shelby said meekly.

"Speak up child," Mrs. Higgins directed her voice to Shelby looking at her over her cat shaped eye glasses. "We will work on your diction and grammar this year. By the time we are through, you will have learned to project your voice so that others can hear you, and you won't talk like a hillbilly."

"Yes, ma'am."

"Otis Shepherd," Mrs. Higgins went on mercifully leaving Shelby to sink lower in her big wooden desk.

"Here, ma'am," a boy said loudly.

"Kenny Lawson," Mrs. Higgins went on with her roll call.

"Here, ma'am."

That's the Kenny from my bus that the big girl pushed out of his seat, I thought. I was wondering how often Big Brenda bullied him, when Mrs. Higgins called out, "I said, Helen Roy."

Everybody was looking at me.

"Oh, I'm here ma'am, but everyone calls me Lizzy."

"Is that so? Well, you were registered in the school office by the name of Helen Roy. I already have that name in my roll book, so you will be Helen in this classroom. I don't care what you call yourself on the playground, but I want Helen Roy written at the top of your papers. Do I make myself understood, Helen?"

"Yes, ma'am," I said looking at Shelby who had turned around with the rest of the class to look at me. Her sad little brown eyes said, "Don't worry, I know how you feel."

"Now let's quit staring at Helen and stand for the pledge," Mrs. Higgins commanded as she stood up next to her desk and faced the flag by the doorway.

I said the pledge out of memory, but my mind was on Grandma Puckett. She would be thrilled that my teacher was calling me Helen and there was nothing I could do about it. Only my relatives and the three boys in Sunday school knew me as Lizzy. All my new classmates would be calling me Helen. Mrs. Higgins would make sure of that. The lessons for the morning were easy for me. I finished my papers quickly. Then I watched as Shelby struggled to do hers.

When Mrs. Higgins had us to come up one at a time and read to her at her desk, Shelby looked like she could melt into the hardwood floor.

"Shelby, you will be in group three," Mrs. Higgins said frowning.

At least she doesn't call her groups by bird names, I thought relieved.

"You will be in group one, Helen," Mrs. Higgins smiled at me after I'd read a page from my reader aloud.

Shelby smiled at me too as I walked back to my desk and mouthed, "Good job, Lizzy."

Just wait, I was thinking. *Soon you'll be reading like me,* but I didn't dare say the words out loud. Talking out of turn was not permitted in Mrs. Higgins' classroom.

At lunchtime, Shelby and I sat at the same table as Kenny and Otis. Kenny showed Otis some scratches on his arm that he said came from Big Brenda on the bus.

"Oh! That Brenda!" Kenny said. "One of these days I'm going to get her back really good."

"Better not," Otis replied. "Next time she's liable to poke you in the eye with those big dagger fingernails. Better just stay away from her and from that guy too."

Otis pointed over to the cafeteria doorway.

"Here he comes," said Shelby looking nervously down at her food as Jacob Harley headed our way.

"Well, if it isn't the bluebird and the woodpecker," Jacob taunted as he stood by our table. "Better watch out for the new girl, boys. That redhead has a mean streak."

"Helen ain't mean, Jacob," said Kenny.

"Who's Helen?" Jacob asked. My face started to turn red and I shook my head back and forth at Kenny, but he didn't get the point.

"This here's Helen, Helen Roy, all the way from Indiana," Kenny informed Jacob.

Jacob laughed. "Well, now, I've heard of Helen of Troy, but I've never heard of Helen of Roy. What do you know?"

Oh, great, I thought. *Now, he'll be calling me Helen of Roy every chance he gets.*

It wasn't long until my prediction came true. Recess was a half-hour of torment for Shelby and me. If he wasn't teasing her, he was coming at me about my red hair or my name.

"Shelby, we're going to have to find out something about that boy so we can hold it over his head."

"I don't know anything except that he's mean," she said quietly. "Oh, and his daddy drinks a lot. I hear tell that sometimes he gets pretty mean to Jacob and his mama too."

🖋   🖋   🖋

Well, drinking too much making a person mean; that I understood. My mom and daddy could get pretty mad at each other when they were drinking. Sometimes they'd even yell at me.

Grandpa and Grandma Roy drank a little, but they didn't seem to have a problem with it. They drank at the Legion Hall but not at home. Grandpa said drinking was for socializing. In your own home you shouldn't need alcohol to be sociable. But there was this one World War II veteran named Dave who drank all the time. I would laugh at him when he'd get a little tipsy, as Grandma Roy called it, because he did silly things. But one time he scared me. He yelled at Grandpa Roy and even pulled his fist back like he was going to hit him in the face, just because Grandpa Roy said maybe he'd had enough and ought to go home.

"Who made you my judge?" he screamed at Grandpa Roy. "You sound like my wife; always thinking I ought to be home instead of here with my buddies who really understand me. If you think I ought to go home, then you're no buddy of mine."

Then he called Grandpa some names that had cuss words in them, and I saw the hurt in Grandpa Roy's face.

I felt sad when Grandpa was quiet on the way home, even though Grandma tried to help him think of other things and not worry about what Dave had said.

"Oh, put the skids on it, Ruby," Grandpa said sharply. Then Grandma got mad and she wouldn't talk the rest of the night.

Yeah, I knew how drinking could make people mean. But that didn't excuse Jacob Harley. He was the kind of kid that Grandpa would say needed a "knot jerked in his tailpipe." I'd been yelled at lots of times when my parents were drinking, but I didn't think it turned me into a bully. Maybe it was because I could always run over to Grandma and Grandpa Roy's house and feel loved. I was still thinking on all of this when I got on the bus to go home. I made sure that I sat with Shelby and the two of us were nowhere close to Big Brenda. She was another bully who needed someone to put her in her place, but I wasn't going to be the one to do it. That didn't mean I couldn't give Kenny some good ideas.

CHAPTER 13

Grandma was waiting for me when I got off the bus. She was in the kitchen making homemade bread. She sliced me off a piece and spread homemade strawberry jam on it. Grandpa was coming in the back door from milking Fern.

"Hey, slice me off some of that too. I've got the milk to wash it down with."

"Both of you better be washing up," Grandma said, directing me to the sink.

"How'd your day go, Lizzy?" Grandpa asked.

"Ok, but Mrs. Higgins is pretty mean. She called me Helen Roy and said I had to use that name on all of my work."

"Well, now, Helen is a beautiful name," Grandma said handing me a slice of bread. "Did you know that Helen was my mother's name?"

"No," I bit into the soft homemade bread.

"Yes, she was Helen Binder before she married my daddy. Then she became Helen Hanson."

"So you were Mildred Hanson before you married Grandpa Puckett?" I was delighted to find out some of my family's history.

"Sure was. I was so happy when I got a letter from your Grandma Roy that Marjorie had named you Helen.

It made me think maybe she hadn't forgotten all of us after all."

"You and Grandma Roy wrote to each other?" I could hardly imagine it.

"Oh, a few times, only when my letters kept coming back unopened. Then I wrote to your Grandma Roy and asked her why Marjorie and Jason weren't getting my letters. I thought maybe they'd moved again. She wrote me back and said they were still there in Indianapolis and maybe they were just too busy with their new baby, Helen Louise." Grandma got a lump in her throat and little pools formed in her bottom eyelids.

"So you see, Helen, from that day on, I thanked God for you and started praying I'd get to see you someday. I even got your name put on the ladies' prayer bridge. We've all been taking the name of Helen Roy to the throne of grace for the last ten years. And at long last our prayers have been answered."

"Wow! This Grace lady is so good she's got her own throne?"

"What are you talking about?" Grandpa asked.

"That girl, Grace, Grandpa. The one in the song who saved that guy who thought he was bad enough to be a wrench."

Then Grandpa laughed so hard his round tummy was shaking and Grandma had to use her apron to dry away tears that were falling down her cheeks. I didn't know what was so funny.

"Why are you laughing at me Grandma and Grandpa?"

"Oh Honey, we're not laughing at you," Grandpa said. "It's just that grace is not a person."

"She's not?" I asked with a puzzled look on my face.

"No, grace is something from God. It's when God loves us when we ain't worth loving. It's got to do with God sending his Son to die for us when we ain't worth dying for. It's like getting a present when you don't deserve one. That's what grace is."

"Oh, I almost forgot," Grandma said pulling an envelope from her apron pocket. "You got a letter today from your Grandma Roy. Hope it is good news."

I took the letter from Grandma and tore it open right there. When I finished the first page, I looked up at Grandma and Grandpa and asked, "Where is Vietnam?"

CHAPTER 14

I couldn't wait to see Shelby the next day. I fairly flew to the bus. Making sure I said, "Hi!" to Uncle Don, I took my place beside Shelby and began to tell her about Grandma Roy's letter.

"I got a letter from my Grandma Roy in Indianapolis yesterday," I told Shelby.

"Did she say she missed you? Did she tell you anything about your mama or daddy?"

"That's the part that's not so good. Mom hasn't written her or Grandpa Roy since she left. She hasn't written Daddy, and she hasn't written to me like she said she would. It's kind of scary with her being in New York and nobody knowing how to get a hold of her."

"I'll bet that didn't set too well with Grandma and Grandpa Puckett.

"I guess it upset them pretty badly because after I told them about the letter, Grandma said she had a headache and was just going to lie down for a while. She picked up Daisy and her Bible and went to her bedroom. She didn't come out again until supper time, and then her eyes were all red and puffy. Grandpa said he was going to check on the animals in the barn, but he'd just come in from milking Fern. He said I could help him, but he had this sad look in his eyes, so I told him I had homework to do."

"What did the letter say about your daddy?"

"Daddy said he wanted to go to far away places when he reenlisted in the army. Well, I guess he got his chance. But when I told Grandma and Grandpa Puckett that Daddy had been sent to Vietnam, they acted like it was a bad thing. I thought they'd be happy he was seeing the world, but they just looked sadder than before."

"I've heard about Vietnam, Lizzy. It's a place that lots of our soldiers are going to. Mama and Daddy talk real quiet about it when they think us kids are asleep 'cause Ted's almost 18 and Mama's afraid he'll get sent there. There's a draft you know. All the 18 year old boys have to go. But daddy tells her not to worry about it because we're conscientious objectors."

"What's that?"

"That means we don't believe in going to war, or having anything to do with fighting, or killing, or nothing like that."

"Oh," I said suddenly remembering that my mom had married a soldier. "Does that mean that Grandma and Grandpa Puckett are conscientious objectors too?"

"Yep! Everybody in our church is one. We ain't supposed to fight."

"Not even if Big Brenda tries to stab us with her fingernails," I said as we pulled up beside the rundown shack and Big Brenda sauntered to the bus.

"Not even then."

We both scooted closer to the window as Big Brenda grabbed Kenny out of his seat again and sent him sprawling to the floor dropping his books.

"Take a seat," Uncle Don shouted, looking up into the rear view mirror, at Kenny bending over in the middle of the aisle.

"Does Kenny go to your church?" I asked.

"No, he's a Baptist."

Later in the day, I had an idea come to me during art class that could help Kenny with Big Brenda. I told him my idea and he seemed anxious to try it out. I didn't tell Shelby my idea. It didn't seem like something a person from her church would approve of, but since Kenny was a Baptist, and didn't object to war, I figured it was time he defended himself against the enemy. By the time we got back on the bus, Kenny was equipped for battle.

Kenny knew where Big Brenda would probably sit; right behind the two high school boys, so he sat in the seat right behind her. He waited until Brenda put her hand up on the seat in front of him. She dangled the lethal, bright red nails that looked an inch long as she flirted with the boys. Then Kenny quietly took out the shiny new pair of pointy scissors I'd given him from my art box and cut off two of Brenda's long fingernails before she even knew what happened to her. Brenda gave out a war hoop and picked up Kenny by the front of his shirt. She lifted him over into her seat scissors and all. Just before she could clobber him, Uncle Don slammed on the brakes throwing Kenny out of her grasp into the aisle, and I heard Big Brenda say, "Who is Lizzy Roy?" Then I remembered that Grandma Roy had written my name on my scissors with a permanent laundry marker.

CHAPTER 15

Uncle Don walked with me to the door of Grandma and Grandpa's house. He handed Grandma the scissors and said I had some talking to do. Then he got back on the bus and left me there to explain myself. I told Grandma and Grandpa all about Big Brenda and how she treated Kenny. I told her about the scratch marks on his arms. I told them that I was just trying to help Kenny out, but that it had backfired and now Big Brenda hated me just as much as she did Kenny. And all the time I was talking, Grandma and Grandpa were quietly sitting at the kitchen table. I steeled myself for the shouts or even the wooden spoon. I knew I deserved it for taking matters into my own hands instead of just telling Uncle Don what was going on.

"Lizzy," Grandpa said firmly. "You will go up and sit in your room to think about your actions today, until Grandma and I decide on your punishment."

Relieved that there was no yelling, I said, "Yes, sir," and went up to my room. I sat on the bed and thought about what punishment they might give me. Surely this was worthy of a spanking with the wooden spoon, because I had not only gotten back at Brenda, but I had used Kenny, getting him in a fix. Big Brenda would really have it out for him now.

But the longer I sat there, the more upset I became. Hadn't I already had enough punishment since I'd been here in Tennessee? I was a million miles away from my mom and daddy. I'd been snatched from Grandma and Grandpa Roy who loved me like their own child to live with relatives I didn't know. I was forced to wear these ugly, scratchy clothes and shoes that pinched while other girls in the school wore knee length dresses and saddle oxfords. I had to endure three services of church a week and a Sunday school where Jacob Harley tried to make my life miserable. By the time I heard my name called from the kitchen, I had convinced myself that I really didn't deserve a punishment. I'd been punished enough.

"Helen, come to the kitchen please," Grandma called up the stairway.

I went to the kitchen and found Grandma laying out flour, sugar, eggs, and butter. Grandpa's chair was empty.

Maybe he's gone to get a switch, I thought.

"Have you ever made sugar cookies?" Grandma asked.

"No, ma'am," I answered not telling her that my mom wouldn't let me get near the oven when she wasn't home for fear I'd burn the apartment down. And when she was home, she was too tired or angry to teach me to bake anything.

"Well, I think it's time you had a lesson in making cookies."

What is this? I wondered, *My last meal?*

"Come over here and watch while I make this first batch. Then you are going to make a batch of your own."

Grandma wrapped one of her big aprons around my middle overlapping the strings around the front and then tying them in the back. I watched and tried to remember how she'd read the recipe and measured the ingredients. She put the completed ball of dough over to the side on some flour and led me through the process again, but this time I did all the measuring and stirring. Finally I had a ball of dough that looked like Grandma's.

"Now we're going to roll this out pretty thin and cut out some shapes."

She pulled a heart shaped cookie cutter out of the drawer and several cookie sheets. Rolling it out was the hard part, but with each section of dough, it got easier. When we were finished, we had four cookie sheets full of little heart shaped cookies covered with red sugar sprinkles ready for the oven. I was really feeling proud of myself. I couldn't wait for the first batch to come out of the oven so I could taste one. My very first homemade cookies! Wouldn't Mom have been proud of me?

When the first cookies came of the oven, I asked, "Can I taste one of them, Grandma?"

"May I taste one of them?"

"May I taste one of them, Grandma?"

"No, these cookies aren't for you."

"Who are they for?"

"These cookies are going be divided up and given to the people you have hurt. These cookies are for Kenny, Uncle Don, and Brenda Bower."

"But Grandma, I worked so hard to make these!"

"Yes, and you worked pretty hard contriving a way to hurt Brenda. In the meantime, you hurt Kenny and you put undo stress on your Uncle Don. Now he's got to be watching out hard so that the three of you don't hurt each other any more."

I hung my head knowing that what she said was true.

"I suggested you get a good whipping, but this was your Grandpa's idea. It pains me that your mama must not have taught you the Golden Rule, so this is how you're going learn it. Now go and get me three little strawberry baskets off of the back porch and we'll divide these up and take them to their houses."

"What if Brenda throws them back in my face?"

"We can't make people forgive us. All we can do is try to make it a little easier for them find it in their hearts to do it."

CHAPTER 16

It had been a month since we dropped off the cookies at Brenda's broken down shack. I found out it was just her and her daddy living there. No wonder she was so wild. She needed a mother. She was still mad at me on the bus, but she never touched me. Uncle Don made sure of that. I was still enduring Jacob's taunting at school and at church, but I'd made up my mind that I wasn't going to take the matter into my own hands like I had with Brenda. I didn't know how long Grandpa could keep Grandma from using the form of punishment she suggested, "a good whipping." Still, not only did I have to see Jacob every day at lunch and recess, now Shelby and I had to endure his teasing at the Revival Meeting at Promise Falls Church of God. Already they'd had a week of meetings, and there was one more week to go.

Our whole routine was different during revival. After school, I had to hurry with my homework because supper would be at 4:30 on the dot. Grandpa didn't want indigestion to hamper his preaching, so he had to eat early enough to let his food digest. Then everyone changed clothes, putting on their Sunday best, and hopped into the truck to get there early enough for Grandpa to shake hands at the door with all the new folks who came in from the neighboring areas. Each night, the little church was packed, as revival was somewhat of a community event to be looked forward to. At least that was what I was told. The only part of revival I enjoyed was getting to sit with Shelby.

After the singing and praying at the beginning of the service, Grandpa would get up and ask for testimonials. People would stand and say how God had worked wonders in their lives, sicknesses healed, food or money provided in some mysterious way, and even prodigal children brought home again. It seemed that Grandma would dab at her eyes extra hard when these last testimonials were given and I wondered if she was thinking of my mom.

Then the preaching would begin in earnest. Grandpa would pour out everything he had on his heart. Holding his Bible high in the air, he would beg the people to turn their lives over to the Lord. The more excited he got, the louder he preached. His face got bright red as he paced the front of the stage. Taking short gasps between sentences, I wondered how he could even breathe at all. I could feel my heart going up in my throat and my muscles tightening, wishing he would calm down and take a good breath.

I was always relieved when he would reach for his hymnal on the side of the pulpit and ask everyone to stand and sing the invitation song. My favorite one was "Just as I Am" because it was slow and pretty. And besides that, it only had three verses, though sometimes we'd sing those three verses each through twice. If somebody did come forward during the invitation, you knew you'd be singing all the verses again and maybe a third time if someone else walked down the aisle. In the first week of revival I had seen five people come forward; practically one each night.

After the last amen, if there'd been a decision, everyone would tramp out the front door of the church and walk as a group to Promise Falls. There Grandpa and the sinner would get down in the pool at the bottom of the falls and Grandpa would do the baptism quickly because there was getting to be a "nip in the air" as Grandma called it and the water was pretty chilly. A couple of the deacons would wrap the new Christian in towels when they stepped up out of the pool, and get them back to the church to get dried off.

All of this holy activity started to have some effect on me. I was starting to think maybe God was watching down on us, and maybe he even saw Helen Louise Roy. Then came the night when my tender shoot of faith was just about trampled to the ground.

☙ ☙ ☙

It was the last night of revival and Grandpa had been praying all week that certain people would show up and be saved. One of those people walked into the church that night surprising all of us. Mr. Harley stumbled into the back row, drunk as a skunk.

I knew something strange had happened the moment Jacob's dad walked into the church. We were on the last of the opening songs when every head in the house looked towards the back row. I didn't know Jacob's dad, but I could smell him. I couldn't tell you how many times I'd smelled the same thing in my own house when my mom or dad would come home drunk. Grandpa knew who had come just in and slouched down on the back row by the aisle, and he got very excited; so excited that he forgot all about testimonial time and went right into his sermon.

Grandpa preached with fervor. He got red in the first two sentences. If Jacob's dad started to close his eyes, Grandpa would just shout louder, or slam the palm of his hand down on the pulpit emphasizing his point. The longer he preached and gasped for breath, a little fear began to grow in my brain. I decided I could try to pray because my fear was about Grandpa. I wasn't used to praying, and wasn't really sure how to start out even though I'd heard a lot of praying going on for the last two weeks.

"God, this is Lizzy. I know you're not used to hearing from me, but I need to ask you something. It's not for me, God. It's for Grandpa, you know, your special guy whose been doing a lot of your work down here in the Promise Falls Church of God. Please God, don't let Grandpa get sick from not being able to breathe. He's the best preacher you've got around here, so please take care of him and let him get his breath, will you? Thanks, God. I appreciate it."

I felt a little better when I finished my prayer, but Grandpa didn't get any less excited. He was still gasping for breath when he picked up the hymnal a full half hour later than he usually did. Everybody stood and we started singing the invitation hymn, and all the while Grandpa was looking at Mr. Harley and talking straight to him.

"If God has been speaking to you tonight, telling you that he'll forgive you for your sins; don't turn your back on him now. Walk down this aisle into the arms of God," Grandpa pleaded as the music played on.

"He can make you whiter than snow and put a new heart in you, because of what Jesus did for you on the cross. He took your sins on as his own, and threw them as far as the east is from the west, never to remember them no more. So come and ask him to be your Lord and Savior. We don't none of us know how much more time we got on this earth. This just might be the day the Lord calls you home. Will you be ready? What if he calls you right now? Would you be going to heaven with Jesus?"

Then without any warning, Grandpa gave out a groan, clutched at his chest, and fell to the floor while the piano kept on playing.

CHAPTER 17

Grandma sent me home with Shelby that night. Ted drove the station wagon home because Uncle Don and Aunt Betty were at the hospital with Grandma and Grandpa. They'd taken Grandpa to the hospital in Mountain City, Tennessee because Dripping Springs only had Dr. Phillips who was a veterinarian. Fortunately, Dr. Phillips was in the third row that night and realized right away that Grandpa was having a heart attack. He rushed down to the front where Grandpa had fallen. Everybody started getting out of their pews to gather around grandpa, but the deacons told them to back up except for Grandma. They let her stay there crying and praying out loud. Shelby had been sitting next to me. We grabbed each other's hands and stayed in the pew like the deacons told us to. Tears were falling down my face and onto my light blue dress. I looked over at Shelby's lap and her dress was wet with tears too.

Dr. Phillips pushed on Grandpa's chest with the palm of his hand in a steady rhythm, stopping every once in a while to breathe air into grandpa's lungs and see if he had a pulse. After what seemed like a long time, Grandpa coughed and everyone breathed a sigh of relief that he was finally breathing on his own.

Dr. Phillips asked if anybody had a car big enough to take Grandpa to the hospital, and Deacon Fuller said he had a 1965 Cadillac. Grandma got in the passenger side of the front seat, and Dr. Phillips got in the back with grandpa. Uncle Marvin and Aunt Jeannie took Uncle Don and Aunt Betty in their car so Ted would have the station wagon to get their family home. The rest of Grandpa's children got in their cars and followed Deacon Fuller down the road looking a little like a fast moving funeral procession. In my heart, I wondered if it would turn out to be just that before they got to Mountain City.

Shelby and I stood outside with the rest of the congregation watching the vehicles take Grandpa away from us. Then one of the elders, Brother Joe, suggested that we all hold hands and have a prayer circle right there under God's heavens and pray for Grandpa.

"Lord, we know you did a great miracle for us already tonight by starting Brother Henry's heart up again." All around me were "Amen's" and "Hallelujah's" softly spoken by the people who loved Grandpa as much as I did.

"Lord, God, we just ask that you get him to the hospital safe and that you would use the doctors there to bring him back to full health. You know we need him here a little while longer, Lord," Joe prayed with his voice choking and tears coming down his face.

"Yes, Lord, yes," the congregation agreed. We cried rivers of tears. I wanted to wipe my nose, but I was holding Shelby's hand on one side and Tim's on the other side.

Then the man beside Joe began to pray aloud. When he was finished, the person next to him took over. All around the circle, the adults prayed with heads down, until someone spoke that made everyone look up to see who was talking.

"Lord, I know you were using the preacher to talk to me tonight. I heard you telling me to come forward and I held back. So you tried to show me what my stubbornness could cost me. You wanted me to see what was going happen to me if I didn't quit following that demon drink and let you be the Lord of my life. Well, now Lord, I'm getting the message loud and clear, and I'm asking you to come in and make me that new creature that the preacher said you was able to do. And God, please save the preacher's life, because I'm going to need his and your help if I'm going to make it in this new life. Forgive me, Lord. I'm begging you, please."

When Mr. Harley finished his prayer, a new wail went up from his wife and the other members of the congregation, but it was a cry of joy. Brother Joe ended the prayer circle and immediately, everyone congregated around Mr. Harley patting him on the back and assuring him that they'd be praying for him. Then we all walked down to Promise Falls and watched Mr. Harley die to the old life and rise to the new one as he went under the water and came back up.

"We'd best be concluding this service, before Ed here freezes to death," Brother Joe said.

"Well, at least I'd know where I was going if I did," Ed Harley said and everyone laughed.

It felt good to laugh but as soon as we all got in the station wagon to go to Uncle Don's house, a gloom settled over me. What would I do without Grandpa around to keep Grandma "evened out" as I'd heard Shelby say one time? How could anyone really know what would happen to him there in the hospital? What if he didn't make it? And more important than that, how could I believe God would hear all of those prayers when He hadn't heard mine?

🖋   🖋   🖋

Shelby's big sisters made me up a bed on their living room couch and even let Shelby sleep on blankets on the floor beside me. I guess they thought I was pretty shook up, because I wasn't talking; not even to Shelby. But really I was just plain mad; mad at God. After I had just tried praying for the very first time in my life, and asked God to help Grandpa be able to breath, what good did it do? I might just as well been talking to a brick wall.

"Lizzy," Shelby called to me from her bed on the floor after her sister had turned out the living room lights making the room too dark for me to see her face.

"Yes,"

"You want to pray with me about Grandpa?"

"No, you go ahead if you want to. God and I aren't on speaking terms right now. I'm not even sure there is a God out there."

"Oh, Lizzy, surely you don't mean that, do you? How can you say that? There really is a God and he's looking out after Grandpa right now."

"Well, he's got a funny way of showing it."

"Grandpa says that when two people pray together, God is right smack in the middle of them, so please pray with me, Lizzy. It's important to talk to God when some-one you love is sick or hurting."

"Well, then pray for me too, because I'm sick and tired of this religion stuff, and I want to go back to Indiana where I can be normal."

Shelby let out a little whimper, and I knew she was crying into her pillow. I hated myself for making her cry, but the words had already come out of my mouth, and I didn't know how to take them back.

"Dear Jesus," Shelby began to pray aloud between sobs. "Please heal Grandpa's heart and make him all better. We need him, Jesus, awful bad. And Jesus, please reach out and touch my best friend and cousin, Lizzy. Show her that you're real, God, and help her to know how much we love her here in Dripping Springs. In Jesus' name, Amen."

Shelby sniffed a few more times, and then I heard her soft breathing as she drifted off to sleep. I stayed awake looking up at the stars that had started to peek through the clouds out through the lacy living room curtains.

If God really was up there, maybe he just didn't listen to girls like me who had big doubts about who he really was and what he had the power to do. But deep inside of me, I hoped he would listen to Shelby who talked to him like he was her best friend.

CHAPTER 18

I was hoping that Sunday church services would be suspended the next day since the preacher was in the hospital, but Stacy woke Shelby and me up and told us to get ready for church the next morning.

"How will we have church without Grandpa?" I asked Shelby.

"Brother Joe will probably fill in," she guessed and she was right. Everything just went right on like nothing had happened. People were singing and smiling, and I just wanted to scream.

"What is the matter with these people? How can they be so calm? Don't they understand that Grandpa's had a heart attack? Why isn't somebody worried about that? Why aren't we all running to the hospital to be with Grandma?"

Then, during the prayer time, Brother Joe said he had some news for all of us.

"I just came back from the hospital this morning, before the service started," he said. My heart was in my throat and I couldn't breathe.

"I want y'all to know that Brother Puckett's doing real fine. Those doctors are dumbfounded over there at the hospital. They did one of them newfangled bypass surgeries on him last night, and they said he was doing much better than they expected. They said the way he's going, he'll be home before you know it. His heart doctor said he cheated death, but we all know what really happened. God heard our prayers and gave Brother Henry back to us. Amen, brothers and sisters?"

Everyone shouted, "Amen!" and started clapping and praising God. I exhaled and breathed in hard. Shelby grabbed my hand and squeezed it.

"See, Lizzy," she said. "There is a God, and he heard our prayers."

I had to admit, it did seem that something big had happened, but I really didn't know if God had a hand in it until I went to the hospital a few days later to see Grandpa.

"Come on in here, Lizzy," Grandpa said as I stood at the door of his room. "Sit down here by my bed and talk with me a spell."

"How are you, Grandpa?" I asked looking at the strange tubes in his arms and nose.

"Aw, I'm just doing fine, Honey," he said smiling at me. "You see, God's been telling me to slow down for some time now, but I just wasn't listening too good. I guess He thought I ought to take a breather for just a little while, and I'm going to have to do it whether I want to or not. Yep, I'm just going to take me a big breath and have a little vacation at home with you and Grandma. Is that all right with you?"

"It's all right with me," I said squeezing his hand while big tears rolled down my cheeks. "It sure is all right with me."

CHAPTER 19

Our Sweet Little Lizzy,

Thanks for writing about your Grandpa Puckett's heart surgery. We're so glad to hear he's better, but how are you holding up down there? It's everything I can do to keep Grandpa Roy from borrowing Sam Morgan's motor coach and going down there to bring you back here to Indiana. I keep telling him that the judge will put him in contempt if he does. I remind him and myself too, that Christmas is coming, but we're both worried sick about you. You keep writing and let us know what's going on down there, and we'll let you know the news from up here.

We're glad you're getting along so well in school and with your cousin, Shelby. She seems like a really nice little girl. I guess I always knew you needed a best friend your own age.

Talking about best friends, I just have to tell you what your Grandpa Roy's best friend, Charlie, did this past weekend. He bit into an apple and his right front tooth came out. Your grandpa kept telling him to get to the dentist, but you know how tight he holds onto his money. Well, instead of going to the dentist, he went down into his basement and mixed up some epoxy glue and glued that tooth right up against his other front tooth. Can you believe it? It's been holding for the last week! It didn't even fall out when he ordered a steak, but he's not trying it out on apples or corn on the cob for a while. He doesn't want to push his luck.

Talking about luck! I won $5.00 last night in the slot machine down at the Legion Post at Speedway. I'm beginning to think the machine at our post is rigged. I haven't won anything out of that one ever since you left. Maybe that's it. Maybe I lost my good luck charm when I lost you Honey Girl.

Well, no use crying over spilled milk. Christmas will be here before you know it. Write us whenever you can. We love you, Lizzy.

Grandma Roy

P.S. I saw your mom on T.V. the other night. She was in New York City all right, but she wasn't in any Broadway play. She was standing in Times Square with a bunch of those hippies protesting the war in Vietnam. She was holding up a big sign that said, "Make Love Not War." You don't have to tell your Grandma and Grandpa Puckett this part. It'd probably kill them to know what kind of life Maggie's living. And if I wasn't holding your Grandpa Roy back, he'd go to New York right now and give her a piece of his mind.

Love and kisses,
Grandma Roy

CHAPTER 20

Thanksgiving Day was here, and at 8:00 in the morning, I was still in bed feeling down in the dumps. I had every reason to be happy and thankful. I had today and Friday off from school. Grandpa Puckett was pretty much healed up from his heart surgery. He was even back to preaching, but he went slower and paced himself now. I could smell the turkey in the oven.

Grandma had been spending the last two weekends teaching me to bake special family recipes; holiday goodies stored away in tins that would be shared with the whole Puckett clan. I'd helped Shelby study her spelling words on the bus and watched her make her first A+ on last Friday's test. Mrs. Higgins had even said my Thanksgiving poem, "A Turkey Tale," was the best in the class and hung it outside in the hallway.

Still my heart was heavy. The more I did things anticipating the holiday with my family, the more I missed the family I wanted to see the most, my mom and daddy.

I didn't dare mope around Grandma right now, because Daisy was sick and Doc Phillips said there wasn't much hope. Old age had just caught up with her. Grandma was pampering her with special food and keeping her close to the coal furnace heater grate in the corner of the kitchen floor.

"I'm just praying she makes it 'till after Thanksgiving," Grandma had said last night. "It's hard to lose someone you love during the holidays."

Don't I know it! I thought. And yet I didn't share my heartaches with Grandma who was so stressed over her sick little poodle. Grandma didn't need another thing to worry over.

"Where's Grandpa Puckett?" I asked when Grandma came into my bedroom to get the porcelain pot from under the bed.

"He's out milking Fern. What are you doing lying around on your bed? Are you sick?"

"No, I'm not sick. Just thinking, that's all."

"Missing Shelby already? You two have been joined at the hip ever since you got here. She's coming over for Thanksgiving dinner you know. Cheer up! It's not like the world's ending if you don't see her for a few hours. Do you want to help me make the pumpkin pies this morning?"

"Sure," I said, smoothing out the wrinkles in the bedspread. "I think I'll just go check on Grandpa."

"Ok, but don't forget your hat."

The barn smelled sweet and musty all at the same time; the smell I had come to love. I always had to let my eyes get adjusted to the dim light after coming in from outside.

"Grandpa, are you in here?" I called out.

"Over here, feeding Stubborn," Grandpa answered.

I liked seeing Grandpa back in his bib overalls even if they were baggy. He'd lost a lot of weight the past month after his surgery, since Grandma had been trying to follow doctor's orders and cut back on sweets and fried foods. Still the overalls made him look strong and manly.

"Why'd you name that mule Stubborn?" I asked hoping I might get a good story.

"It's the nature of the beast."

"Is that all?" I asked. "Isn't there a story to go along with that name?"

I remembered that he told me he'd named the cow, Fern, because she swayed like a fern in the wind when she walked.

"Nope," Grandpa answered. "Some creatures are just stubborn by nature, and no amount of coaxing is going to change them. So why not just call them by what they are?"

"Well, then somebody should have named Jacob Harley, Pest."

"Well now, people are different," Grandpa smiled. "They can change their natures. The Bible is full of times when people got their given names changed by God."

"Really?" I said. "Who?"

"Well, there was Abram. He got his name changed to Abraham, and Jacob got his name changed to Israel, and even Simon got his name changed to Peter."

"Yes, well, according to Mrs. Harley, those were all good guys, so how's that fit in with Jacob? Maybe the bad ones can't change."

"Think about what you are saying, Lizzy. Haven't you seen the big change in Ed Harley, Jacob's dad, now that he's quit drinking and is trusting in the Lord? Besides that, don't you remember me telling last Sunday about how God changed a bad guy's name from Saul to Paul? Of course God did have to kick Saul off of his horse and blind him to knock some sense into him and make him come around to God's way of thinking."

"Yes, and it might take a bright light and getting kicked off your horse to knock some sense into Jacob Harley too, Grandpa," I sighed. "He's just downright mean."

"Well, maybe it will take a light; a light that shines from within us to show him the way."

And maybe it might just take him getting bucked off of his high horse, I thought to myself. *And maybe I'll be there to watch it happen.*

Thanksgiving dinner the next day was everything I hoped it would be. All the Puckett clan was there crammed inside of Grandma's house. We had a wonderful meal together and then Shelby and I stole up to my room to get away from the crowd.

"I wish you were going to be here for Christmas break," Shelby sighed. "It's just not going to be the same without you. We always have the big Christmas pageant at church on the Sunday before Christmas and then come back to our house and exchange gifts among the family."

"I'm sure it's fun." I smiled at her. I would have liked to have told her how my heart was aching to see Grandma and Grandpa Roy, and possibly my some of my old friends in Indianapolis, but I didn't want to make her think she wasn't my closest friend in all the world. "I'll miss you something awful," I said really meaning it.

"Well, you won't miss Jacob Harley strutting around all puffed up because he always gets to be the narrator in the church Christmas play. You think he's hard to live with now. It's even worse at tryouts, because he knows he's going to be picked year after year."

"Why don't you try out for it Shelby," I encouraged. "Wouldn't that be something if you got the part this year?"

"I couldn't do it," she sighed. "At tryouts, they bring you out one at a time and give you a piece of paper with the narrator's opening lines on it. You don't get a chance to read it ahead of time and practice. You have to just read it cold. I tried last year, because mama said I'd be perfect for the part, but I stumbled on a couple of words at the tryouts. Jacob tried out after me and he read it perfectly. No wonder he got the part."

"Hum. I think Jacob's luck is about to change."

That Sunday, I asked Mrs. Fuller, who was in charge of the Christmas play at church, if I could possibly read a copy of the play since I wasn't going to be at church for Christmas break.

"This is highly unusual," Mrs. Fuller replied. "Nobody usually sees the play until tryouts. But since you're not going to be trying out, I guess it would be all right."

"Thanks, Mrs. Fuller," I said beaming as I held out my hand for the copy she was getting out of her Sunday school book bag.

"Now promise me this," she said looking me in the eye. "That you will not let any other child, who is going to try out for the play, read this copy ahead of time."

Mrs. Fuller had a death grip on her end of the mimeographed play. If I didn't promise, I wouldn't get it from her.

"I promise that I will not let any other child sit down and read this play before try outs."

"Ok," Mrs. Fuller said releasing her grip. "I hope you enjoy reading it. I wrote it in January last year when we got snowed in with a blizzard. Might as well get a head start, I thought to myself, instead of waiting until October and then being in a panic like I usually am."

"Thanks again, Mrs. Fuller. By the way, when are tryouts?"

"Next Friday," she said cheerfully.

Next Friday? I thought. *I've got a lot of work to do in one week.*

CHAPTER 21

All afternoon I thought about the promise I had made to Mrs. Fuller. I argued with myself, "I said I wouldn't let them sit down with the copy and read it. I didn't say I wouldn't read it to them."

But no matter how much I tried to convince myself that it would be alright to read the opening narrator's lines to Shelby, I kept wondering what would happen to me and to Shelby if somebody found out. And knowing Jacob Harley, he'd get to the bottom of it somehow. And then the wooden spoon might find its way to Shelby and my bottoms. Worrying about that wooden spoon sure could keep a kid out of trouble all right. Then at Sunday night church, an idea hit me "square in the middle of the road" as Grandpa Roy would have said.

Shelby asked me if I would help her with this week's spelling words because she wanted to get another A+. Her mama and daddy had been really proud of her.

"Sure, I'll even throw in some bonus words."

With that I knew how Shelby was going to get that part. I wouldn't have to read it to her. She was going to recognize the words and read it by herself!

I wrote all of the following week's Spelling words on some little strips of paper Grandma gave me, and then I looked for the hardest words in the speech that Shelby would have to read at tryouts; miracle, Bethlehem, magi, frankincense, myrrh, adoration, and Savior. These became Shelby's Christmas bonus words. On the bus, we made a game out of recognizing the words and being able to pronounce them. Then I drilled her on how to see them in her mind and spell them. By Friday, she was ready in more ways than one. After school we slipped into our seat on the bus and she could hardly contain her giggle.

"Lizzy, I made an A+ again in spelling all because of you!" she said smiling.

"No, Shelby, You did it yourself by studying hard, that's all."

"Are you going to the tryouts tonight?"

"I wouldn't miss it," I said trying not to let my secret out. "You are trying out for the narrator aren't you?"

"Now why would I do that? I'll just mess up and Jacob will laugh at me. I'll probably get stuck being a lamb again. Mama kept last year's costume."

"Shelby, you just have to try out for the narrator's part," I said excitedly. I never thought she might not try out for that part. I'd put a lot of work into this plan, and I wanted her to succeed. Besides, it would feel awfully good to see Jacob take a backseat to Shelby.

"I'll think about it," Shelby said. "Ain't it grand that old Daisy lived through the holidays?"

"Yes, it was a good thing she did," I said quietly, but in my mind I was wondering if my plan for revenge was going to make it through the holidays.

"See you tonight." I waved at Shelby as I got off at Grandma's house.

"Bye!" She waved back smiling.

❦   ❦   ❦

"So tonight's the big tryouts," Grandma said as she handed me a cookie and a glass of milk. "Too bad you're not going to be here for the play. You'd have made a great narrator with your good reading skills."

"I'm trying to get Shelby to try out for that part," I said biting into a soft Snicker doodle. "But she says Jacob will laugh at her if she stumbles on a word."

"Better let her make up her own mind about trying out. It's not a good idea to force somebody to do something they know they won't be good at doing. Shelby's just not a strong reader right now, but she will be someday. I know she will."

"Maybe sooner than you think, Grandma. She's been working on her vocabulary really hard. She's getting better every day."

"Well, go and get ready for the practice," Grandma said pushing me from behind. It's almost four o'clock, and they start saying their lines at four-thirty."

❦   ❦   ❦

We got to church just as Mrs. Fuller said, "And who would like to audition for the part of the narrator?"

100

Jacob's hand shot up. "I'll try," he said and then gave Shelby a look that said, "You'd better stay out of my way this year."

Suddenly, Shelby's hand shot up. "I'd like to try too, Mrs. Fuller."

"Wouldn't you rather be a little lamb?" Mrs. Fuller said. "You looked so adorable in your costume last year."

"Yea," Jacob sneered. "Better to be a lamb than to bawl like a sheep when you can't read your part."

"That's quite enough, Jacob. If Shelby wants to try out for the part, then that is up to her. Now, is there anyone else?"

When no one else raised their hand, Mrs. Fuller said, "Let's have you two read one at a time. Shelby, you go first." Then she handed Shelby the script.

Shelby stood up and cleared her throat. I knew she must have been awfully nervous, but I just smiled urging her on.

"Tonight's play is called 'The Miracle of the Magi.' It takes place in Bethlehem, where Jesus our Savior was born. The Magi saw a star in the East and brought gifts of frankincense, gold, and myrrh to Jesus. They fell on their faces in adoration when they found him, but who were these men from the East? Why did they follow the star? Listen as we tell you the story."

I looked around at everyone's faces as Shelby said the lines without missing or stumbling on any of the words. They seemed to be in shock, but Shelby's face was shining like the gold she'd just read about. A smile spread across her face when she shut the booklet and took her seat.

"Why, Shelby, that was wonderful!" gushed Mrs. Fuller. "I couldn't have said it better myself, and I wrote it! Jacob, I hope you don't mind trying for a different part. I think we have our narrator right here."

Jacob's face fell. It turned bright red. "There's no other part I want," he said to Mrs. Fuller with his voice quivering. Then he got up and ran out of the room.

"Oh my," Mrs. Fuller said. "What have I done? I should have at least let him read the part."

Shelby stood up. "He can have the part, Mrs. Fuller. I don't mind being a lamb."

"You don't, Shelby? Well, I'm going to try and catch Jacob before he goes all of the way home." With that she fled from the room.

"What are you saying, Shelby?" I asked as she sat back down by me. "You deserve that part. You read every word of it by yourself. I heard you. You can't just give it back to Jacob."

"Well, Lizzy, if I don't, he might not ever come back to church, and then how will Jacob ever learn what Jesus is really like."

"But you wanted that part," I argued.

"No, I didn't want that part. I just wanted to get back at Jacob and that was wrong. When he was teasing me, I got really sore at him. That's the only reason I tried out for the narrator. Why I'm pretty surprised myself that I read it so well. It's like those words were already in my head, and they just popped out of my mouth."

Just then, Mrs. Fuller and Jacob walked back into the room.

"I'm sorry boys and girls," Mrs. Fuller apologized.

"I acted a little hastily and I should have let Jacob read the narrator's part. Jacob, would you come up and try out for the part?"

Jacob came up and read the script putting all of his heart into it with sincerity. When he was finished, everyone clapped; everyone but me that is. Then the other children tried out for Mary, Joseph, the angel, and the three wise men. There were no tryouts for the lamb or the shepherds, because in this play, they had no lines.

"Well, children, I'll list all the parts, and who got them, on the Sunday school doors on Sunday morning. The first practice will be Sunday night. You are all dismissed."

On the way home, Grandma praised Shelby for doing the right thing and acting out the Golden Rule in person.

There's that Golden Rule again, I thought. *It really takes the fun out of getting even with people.* Well, at least now Jacob knew that Shelby could read and read well.

The following Sunday, Jacob looked at the chart outside the Sunday school room and jumped up and down declaring himself the best narrator, because he had beaten Shelby out of the part. Shelby continued to keep quiet about the sacrifice she had made and wouldn't even let me tell Jacob. It got to where I could hardly stand to be around him, so I quit going to watch the practices.

It's just as well, I thought to myself.

After all, Grandma and Grandpa Roy were coming to pick me up the following weekend, and I'd be back in Indiana for Christmas. For two solid weeks I'd be away from Jacob Harley.

CHAPTER 22

Being back in Indiana was a balm for my little Hoosier soul. Grandma and Grandpa Roy were fit to be tied when they picked me up and saw that I was all decked out in a long sleeved, down to the ankle dress with black stockings and lace up shoes. On the way home, they stopped at a department store and bought me some new outfits. One of them was a pair of corduroy pants and a sweater. Grandma said all the kids in Indiana were wearing corduroy that winter. They also bought me a pair of penny loafers and a bright plaid winter coat. I'd been wearing one of Stacy's hand-me-down coats, because it was too big for Shelby.

"You need some color, Lizzy Girl," Grandpa Roy said as he paid for the coat.

"She needs a haircut too. I'm going to take her to Mary Lou's when I have my appointment on Monday."

"What color are you going to come home with?" Grandpa said laughing about Grandma's previous trips to the beauty parlor. "Try not to make it bright orange this time."

"I wish you'd quit bringing that up, Harold. It was only orange once, and that was two years ago."

"Now this is the color you ought to go for," Grandpa said tousling my hair with his big rough hands. "There's no way they can put this color of red in a bottle."

"I missed you two," I said hugging Grandma.

"We missed you terribly, Lizzy," she said back.

"We sure did," Grandpa said, "We're like an engine without a spark plug when you're not around. How about we find a hamburger place around here somewhere and get you a big order of French fries?"

"Yes, Sir! That would be just fine."

"Well, they did teach her some manners down there," Grandma said poking Grandpa in the ribs.

"But who knows what else they taught her," he said softly to Grandma thinking I couldn't hear.

"They're nice people," I said to Grandpa Roy. "I learned how to bake cookies and cross-stitch and toss hay to a cow. In the spring, Grandpa Puckett says he's going to teach me to milk Fern."

"Child labor, that's what's going on down there," Grandpa grumped.

"No, Grandpa. I want to learn to milk a cow."

"And then what will they be having you to do next, make quilts and pot holders to sell at some tourist stop along the road like the Amish do in Shipshewana?"

"Oh, Grandpa," I tickled his side. "They're not going to make me do that. They're just plain ordinary people. They're not Amish."

"Well, they're like the Amish in one way. They don't defend their country, and that's just un-American."

"Shelby told me they were conscientious objectors, Grandpa. They just don't feel God wants them to kill other people," I explained hoping he'd understand.

"Draft-dodgers is what they are and that don't sit too well with me, Lizzy. When I enlisted in the army, WW II, was already in full swing. I went and did my duty. I didn't like the idea of killing anybody either, but sometimes you have to do things you don't want to do to keep your country free for your children and your grandchildren," Grandpa said giving me a hug as we walked back to the car.

I didn't argue anymore with Grandpa Roy, because I knew how he felt about serving his country. He'd shown me his medals lots of times. One of them was a purple heart. He'd reached the rank of Sergeant Major, and he still fit into his uniform. Every Fourth of July and Veterans Day, he'd put his uniform on and join the rest of the men from his Legion Post in a big parade that went through the middle of downtown Indianapolis. I was pretty patriotic myself. Maybe I took more after my dad than I did my mom.

When we pulled up to Grandma and Grandpa's house, I noticed Grandpa had used only red, white, and blue in his outdoor Christmas lights. It was so like him to do that. Every Christmas I could remember had been spent at this house. I hopped out of the car and ran to the porch. I couldn't wait for them to unlock the door.

I pulled the door open and looked around. Only the lights of the Christmas tree were on. I felt like a kid in fairyland. The Christmas tree was glowing and there were packages underneath it with my name on them. There were stockings on the mantle and a new picture of my daddy in his soldier uniform. He looked so serious, and even more handsome than I had remembered.

No wonder Mom had fallen in love with him. Grandma and Grandpa were bringing in the shopping bags right behind me, so I swallowed hard and tried to get rid of the lump in my throat.

Grandma switched on the light and I plopped down on their couch.

"How about a little T.V. before you go off to bed," Grandpa asked. "*Lawrence Welk* is just about to begin." It seemed like years since I'd watched television. Grandma and Grandpa Puckett didn't have one, but I hadn't really missed it until now as I listened to the big band play and watched the familiar champagne bubbles fill the air.

CHAPTER 23

I woke up the next day half expecting to put on my dress to go to church. It was Sunday after all, but then I remembered where I was. It wasn't that my grandparents didn't believe in God. I knew they prayed for my daddy and probably for me too, but they just didn't believe in organized religion. Grandpa had said a lot of times that churches were where the hypocrites hung out together, and he'd rather hang out with his buddies at the Legion where nobody put on any airs. What you saw was what you got. Today was going to be no different.

We were going to the Legion post around noon for the big Christmas dinner they served each year. Then when the dinner was over, the whole post would go to the Veteran's hospital and sing Christmas carols to the patients there. I was excited about seeing my old friends at the Legion post. Most of Grandma and Grandpa's friends were as old as they were. The Korean War veterans were younger and sometimes they brought their kids to the parties. I was hoping to see some of them today.

🖊 🖊 🖊

"Lizzy Roy, you've grown a foot taller. I just can't believe it's you," Grandma's friend, Shirley, said. Shirley was a regular at the Bingo nights at the post. She could play 20 cards all by herself, and she generally won something every time she played.

Today she was dipping up mashed potatoes behind the serving window. She gave me an extra big portion and then came around the end of the counter and gave me a big hug. I was steering clear of the end of her cigarette. Hugging a smoker could be a dangerous thing, but she was one of grandma's best friends so I let her squeeze me tight.

"Little Lizzy, we've been missing your smiling face around here," she said.

"And I've been missing all of you."

"You know there's the big Christmas Bingo game on Tuesday. Are you going to come and help your grandma like you always used to?"

"Sure, she's going to help me, Shirley," Grandma answered. "She's my good luck charm that's come back. Now you're not going to be the only one getting the prizes. You and Tom come and sit with us after you're done dipping up those spuds. We've got lots of things to talk about."

We sat down at a table with Grandpa's friend, Charley, and his wife Charlene. I tried not to be obvious as I stared at Charley's mouth. Sure enough, you could see something plastic looking smeared across his front two teeth. He looked over at me and gave me a big smile. I smiled back like a dog that's been caught in the toilet bowl and ducked my head back down for more mashed potatoes.

"Charlie, are you going to be able to play the harmonica this year when we go caroling?" Grandpa asked.

"Why wouldn't I?" Charlie asked suspiciously.

"Didn't know if the braces on your teeth would get in the way," Grandpa teased.

"I'm doing quite fine with my teeth, but are you going to be able to walk up and down those VA hospital hallways without getting the urge to lay down in one of the beds and rest like you did last year?" Charlie kidded back.

"You old coot! I wasn't lying down. I was just testing out the beds to see if the VA was treating those boys right."

"Oh, sure!" he laughed. "Lizzy, you'd better watch out for your grandpa. He's got one foot in the grave. Why this little nurse last year asked him if he needed a wheel chair, because he was hobbling around so bad. He told her that if she had a spare one, he'd take it."

"I was just teasing with her, but if you had arthritis as bad as I do, you wouldn't think it was so funny. At least I've got my own teeth."

"Well, thanks to this epoxy, I've got my own teeth too," Charlie answered.

And I've got my old friends back, I thought watching the two of them bicker like school children with circles of cigarette smoke making Christmas wreaths around their heads.

The next day, Grandma took me to Mary Lou's to get my hair cut and permed just like she said she would.

I walked through the door and was shocked to see the big black wig was back on its stand by the hair dryer. You'd have never known it had once been on fire like a blazing rocket.

"Well, if it isn't our little Lizzy!" Mary Lou said and hugged me tightly. "It's so good to have you home."

"I missed you too, Mary Lou. How did you get that wig fixed up? I thought it had burned up last Fourth of July."

"I thought so too," Mary Lou said shaking her head. "But then the most amazing thing happened. Some of the people who read about it in the paper started coming in to the shop to get their hair cut. They said they wanted me to use some of their hair to try and repair it. People from all over were making appointments just so they could say they had some of their hair in that wig."

"Really? That's great!" I said it sincerely, because I still felt guilty about it getting ruined in the first place even though Grandma said I saved Mary Lou's life. She said if I hadn't pulled it off of her head, the toxic fumes of the burning paint might have killed her before the flames got down to her own hair.

"Give her one of those cute Shirley Temple looks," Grandma said.

"Grandma Puckett wouldn't like that," I replied softly.

"Well, Grandma Puckett isn't here right now, Lizzy. It's time you started looking like a normal American girl."

When Mary Lou finished with me, I looked like a girl with a red Afro. When I went to bed that night, it felt like I was sleeping on a fluffy cloud. I closed my eyes and tried to think what Grandma and Grandpa Puckett would say when they saw me, but the smell of Grandma Roy's laundry detergent on the pillowcase was so familiar and comforting, that I couldn't keep my eyes open. I drifted off to sleep with such a big smile on my face, that if I'd had a little bigger nose, you would have thought a clown was under the covers.

CHAPTER 24

"What are we doing today, Grandma?" I asked the next morning when I saw her putting bags of candy on the kitchen table.

"Something you're going to like! This is the day we're packing candy and toys for the boys and girls at the Soldiers' and Sailors' Children's Home. Help me put some of each kind of candy in these tins. We'll take them down to the Legion Hall and add them to the ones the rest of the ladies are bringing. Grandpa is going to take us and Charlene and Charlie down to the Children's Home in Knightstown on Friday night to give them to the children that our Legion post has been supporting all year."

"I remember now. Last year you and your friends knitted each one of the kids a stocking and filled it with candy."

"That's right. This year we thought we'd go with tins and then the kids could keep them to put personal items in after the candy is gone."

"Is Grandpa going to get dressed up like Santa again this year and help pass out the presents?"

"He sure is, Sweetie. And this year you get to go too and watch how excited the kids are when we pass out the gifts. They really appreciate what our Legion family does for them all year."

"I can't wait until Friday, then," I said excitedly.

"Well, then come on. Let's get these tins down to the post, and I'll let you take a peek at the toys before we wrap them up.

Grandma and I put the filled tins of candy in the back of her Buick and took them down to the Legion post. Other Auxiliary ladies were there filling big boxes with toys.

"Why does this box say "Division 20" on the side of it?" I asked Grandma. I was staring at a new Hula Hoop sticking out of the top.

"Division 20 is one of the girls' cottages at the Children's Home. Take a look inside, Lizzy. We've tried to include items a young girl would want to get for Christmas."

I peered into the huge box. "Ooh!" I said, looking at batons with colored ribbons coming out of the ends, porcelain dolls, roller-skates, and board games of all kinds.

"I think you did a pretty good job, Grandma." I winked at her. "I'd be happy with any of these toys."

"Well, I'm glad to hear you say that," Grandma laughed. "Because Santa called me the other day and asked me what you wanted for Christmas. I gave him a list for you, since he didn't have your address in Tennessee, but you'll have to wait until Christmas Day to find out what he decided to pack in his bag."

"I think I've already got what I wanted for Christmas," I said as I wrapped my arms around her thin waist trying to avoid her big rhinestone belt buckle. "Just to be home with you and Grandpa makes Christmas special for me." I meant it too.

On Christmas morning, Grandma fixed pancakes and made me eat breakfast before I could open any of my presents. Just like she had hinted, there were some of the same toys and games that I had seen in the boxes for the kids from the Children's Home. The thought hit me that I was like them because I didn't have a mom and dad to spend Christmas with, but then I thought about how much more fortunate I was. I had Grandma and Grandpa Roy and Grandma and Grandpa Puckett to love me.

There was also a small wrapped box from Grandma and Grandpa Puckett. Inside was a delicate gold cross necklace like I had seen Shelby wearing during the fall revival. Grandma Roy fastened it around my neck and it looked pretty against my new sweater.

We had just cleared away the colorful mounds of wrapping paper from the floor, when there was a knock at the door. Grandma opened the door and two grim-faced soldiers she didn't know were standing there.

"No... No...NO!" Grandma cried and collapsed to the floor sobbing.

Grandpa scooped her up in his arms and invited the men to come in.

"We're so sorry to have to tell you this," they said. "Your son, Jason Roy, has been killed in the line of duty."

CHAPTER 25

It was a quiet ride back to Tennessee. Shelby and I sat in the back seat of Uncle Marvin's car. He had let Grandma and Grandpa Puckett borrow it to come to Indiana for the funeral, so they could bring Shelby with them. I was glad she came, but I didn't want to talk to her just now. I was numb. I had no feeling in my heart and no more tears to cry. All I could do was stare out the window and replay the past week over and over in my mind.

Grandma Roy crying, "It's not fair! He was my only son, my only child. It's not fair."

Grandpa asking the soldiers over and over again, "Are you sure it was Jason Roy, our Jason, who was killed? How did he die? Did he die a hero? Are you sure it was our son, Jason? Do you have his dog tags for proof?"

And there I sat only two feet away unable to move or talk. I wanted my mom. I wanted her to take me in her arms and say it would be all right; that she would take care of me from now on. I needed her right then, and she wasn't there for me. She wasn't there for Daddy; to see his body put to rest, and she wasn't there for Grandma and Grandpa Roy to help ease the pain of losing their only son.

The veterans from the Legion post rallied around Grandpa. They sat with him not saying anything really, just being there for him, letting him know they understood his hurt. And the ladies from the Auxiliary had come to comfort Grandma. They had brought food every day for the last week, but I couldn't eat it. There was a terrible lump in my throat that just wouldn't go away. With it was a bitter taste that made me sick to my stomach.

On the morning after the soldiers came, I couldn't get out of bed. All I could do was cry and ask God why he was punishing me.

Grandma came in to check on me around ten o'clock in the morning. She and Grandpa were going to have to go to the funeral home to make arrangements. The army was shipping Daddy's body back to Indianapolis the next day and decisions had to be made.

"Do you want to go down to the funeral home with us, Lizzy?" she asked me softly.

"No. I don't want to go anywhere. I don't want to see anyone. Grandma, would you call Grandpa Puckett and ask him to pray for me? I think God is really mad at me and I don't know what I've done."

"Hush now, baby," she said cradling me in her arms. "None of this was your fault. I'm going to ask Mary Lou to come over and stay with you while we go to the funeral home. This is her day off, and she wants to help me in some way. And Honey, I'll call your Grandpa Puckett. I could use some prayers too."

Grandma and Grandpa Puckett told Grandma Roy that they would leave and head to Indiana the first thing the next morning. They asked her for the nearest hotel to where we lived.

"Don't you even think of staying in a hotel," Grandma had said. "You're staying right here in our house. We have an extra room and people have brought in so much food there is no way we can eat it all by ourselves. Please, stay with us and bring Lizzy's little cousin named Shelby. Lizzy writes about her all the time in her letters. It might help her to have someone younger around that she could confide in. She's not talking much to us, and she's not eating. Please, come soon. We don't know how to comfort her."

True to their word, Grandma and Grandpa Puckett and Shelby showed up the next afternoon. When they walked into the house, I was sitting on the couch looking at Grandma and Grandpa Roy's photograph album. It had pictures of my dad from the time he was a baby. I was looking for a picture of Daddy that I could keep with me. The picture of him in his army suit, from Grandma and Grandpa's fireplace mantel, would be used at the funeral home. Grandma Puckett looked at me in disbelief when she saw my short curly hair and blue jeans. She opened her mouth to say something, but Grandpa quickly squeezed her arm.

"Mildred," he said. "It will grow. Right now she just needs your love." And love me they did. They stayed right beside me during the viewing and the funeral. They prayed with me when they tucked Shelby and me into the double bed we were sharing.

Still my heart was as heavy as a stone. I didn't want to talk. I only ate when they pushed me to eat something. Even Shelby couldn't cheer me up, though she tried.

"The Christmas play turned out real nice," Shelby said. "You should see how Jacob is treating me now since Mrs. Fuller told him that I took the part of the lamb so that he could be the narrator. I guess she got tired of him strutting around like a peacock. He hasn't teased me even once since you left on vacation. He even asked me to help him practice his lines. And the night we gave the play, he said I was the best lamb he'd ever seen."

"I'm glad Jacob is changing his attitude towards you, Shelby," I said. Then I rolled over on my side away from her so she couldn't see my tears. My life just kept changing for the worse.

🐑 🐑 🐑

We got back to Dripping Springs late on Saturday night. As we passed Promise Falls, I saw that there was no water falling from the top. It was like someone had turned the falls off.

That figures, I thought. *The water has dried up, just like my heart.*

Later, at Grandma's house, I passed the place where Daisy should have been sleeping by the back door, but she wasn't there. Her rug wasn't even there.

"Did you have to take Daisy over to Shelby's so they could watch her while you were gone?" I asked on my way up the stairs.

Grandma was right behind me carrying a container I'd gotten from Grandma and Grandpa Roy. They had given me a small box of my daddy's things like his dog tags and other personal effects. They told me I'd want them when I was older, but now I didn't have the heart to even look at them.

"I didn't want to tell you this after all you've been through," Grandma said. "But Daisy died of old age right after you left for Indianapolis. We buried her out by the barn. Maybe tomorrow I can show you the place."

My bed felt comfortable and smelled familiar like a place a person could call home, but inside I felt like an orphan, and I didn't see any hope for my future to look any brighter.

CHAPTER 26

The next day was Sunday, and I didn't want to go to church. I just wanted to stay in bed under the covers and never come out. Grandma came up to help me get dressed, and I told her I didn't feel well.

"I think I caught something in Indiana."

"And I know what it was," Grandma said. "I think you caught a case of the blues, and I don't blame you, but talking with the Lord is the best kind of medicine. Believe me, I know."

When I didn't come down later, Grandpa came up to see me too.

"Lizzy, Grandma says you don't feel well. Is that the truth?"

I didn't want to lie to Grandpa. "I don't feel sick in my stomach," I said. "I feel sick in my heart. I miss my daddy, and I don't think I'll ever see my mom again."

"Thanks for being honest with me, Lizzy, and because of that, I'm going to make an exception to my rule about you being at church every time the doors are open. I need to get on over there to preach, but Grandma is going to stay here with you. You two can have your own little service right here. God doesn't just talk to people in the church building. He's everywhere around us ready to talk and to love."

"Thanks, Grandpa. I'll be there Wednesday for sure."

"I know you will. Now why don't you get dressed and go down and have some breakfast. Grandma has fixed your favorite things."

He kissed me on the forehead, and I could still smell his earthy fragrance, from milking Fern, for minutes after he'd left the room.

After breakfast, Grandma and I had our own little church service in the living room. We sang some hymns from the hymnal she kept at home to practice with at the piano. Then Grandma read a scripture from the book of Isaiah in the Bible.

"Can a mother forget her baby and have no compassion on the child she has borne? Though she may forget, I will not forget you! See I have engraved you on the palms of my hands; your walls are ever before me. Those who hope in me will not be disappointed."

Grandma took my hand. "I'm going to pray for you, Lizzy, like I have prayed for you every day since you were born, but this time I want you to hear the words that I have been praying for the past ten years."

"Okay, Grandma," I said, relieved that she wasn't asking me to pray.

"Dear Heavenly Father," Grandma began. "Please keep this precious grandchild of mine, Helen Roy, in the palm of your hand. Protect her, shield her, and draw her to yourself. And if you see fit, Lord, please find a way to bring her and her mama back to Tennessee where I can hold them and love them. In Jesus' name, Amen."

"Does God always answer your prayers?" I asked.

"Yes, he always answers prayers, but the answer is not always yes. Some times it is, "No," and sometimes it is, "Wait.""

❧ ❧ ❧

I didn't want to go to school the next morning, but I didn't think Grandpa was going to let me stay home from that too, so I got up and got ready for the day. Uncle Don gave me a hug when I got on the bus. Shelby smiled as I sat in the seat next to her.

"I missed you at church yesterday. We all did."

"I wasn't feeling up to it." I confessed. "I knew everyone would have to hug me and tell me they were sorry about my dad."

"That's only because they love you."

"I know," I said. "I guess I'll be ready for it by Wednesday night church. I just hope they still love me when they see my hair!"

"Oh, don't worry about that, Lizzy," Shelby laughed. "By the end of today, every kid will go home and talk about your hair to their parents. By Wednesday, it will be old news."

Shelby got me caught up on all the school news, and by the time the bus pulled up out front, I was almost my old self again. In the morning we wrote about our Christmas vacations, and Mrs. Higgins said I could just write about anything I wanted. She, and everyone else it seemed, had heard about my father's death. Everyone was kind to me, even Jacob Harley.

"Hey, Helen, I like that new hairdo," Jacob said walking towards Shelby and me at recess.

Here it comes, I thought.

"Sorry you missed seeing the Christmas play. I never would have done so well on my part if it hadn't been for Shelby here helping me with my lines. You know in the spring, we have a school play. I hope the two of you will try out for it. We could have a lot of fun together learning our lines." Shelby and I stood there with our mouths open in disbelief. Was this the same Jacob Harley?

"Well, I've got to go," Jacob said backing away from us. "The guys will wonder what I'm doing over here talking with a couple of pretty girls."

As soon as he got out of earshot, Shelby and I looked at each other and burst out giggling.

"Who was that?" I asked.

"That's what I've been trying to tell you. He's been acting different ever since the Christmas play."

"What do you know? Maybe the Golden Rule really does work."

"Or maybe he's just seeing what a difference Jesus can make in a person's life," Shelby said. "His daddy's been sober for three months now, and I hear he's going to some A.A. meetings over in Mountain City. He's even been taking Mrs. Harley over there with him 'cause mama said they've got meetings for the wives too."

"Well, I don't know what's making him different, but I hope it continues."

❦ ❦ ❦

In the afternoon, we started on something new in Math called long division. I liked to work with numbers, and caught on to it right away. On the way home, I helped

Shelby get her homework started on the bus. I tried to explain the circular motion of the numbers in long division as she tried to divide six into four hundred forty-four.

"Start at the top, Shelby," I instructed. "Ask yourself how many times 6 can go into 44 and write that number at the top." Shelby wrote a 7 at the top of the division sign.

"Very good, Shelby. Now work your way down again by asking, 'What is 6 times 7?' and write it under the 44." Shelby wrote 42 under the 44.

"You're doing so well," I said with a smile. "Now subtract. What do you get?"

"I get a 2."

"That's right. Now bring down the other 4 you have left over under the division sign and ask yourself a new question; 'How many times can 6 go into 24?'"

"It goes 4 times," Shelby answered.

"I think you've really got those times tables memorized well! Put the 4 at the top and the 24 under the other 24. When you subtract, you will have nothing left over, and the answer to the problem is 74."

"You make it look so easy," Shelby said. "You'd make a great teacher, Lizzy."

"Do you really think so?"

"Sure do! Why you explained this better to me than Mrs. Higgins. And you're good at school work. You're always making A's on all of your papers."

I'd never thought of being a teacher before. In fact, I'd never even allowed myself to think past this 5th grade year. I had always loved school. It kept my mind off of everything else that was wrong with my life. It was the only place where I had some control over what happened to me. I could choose to learn and make good grades, which I often did. Suddenly I saw a picture of myself as a grown up person. Maybe Lizzy Roy did have a future. Of course if I was a teacher, I would be Miss Roy, or even Miss Helen Roy. Suddenly I forgot to be sad. I even let a little smile come on my face thinking about the possibilities.

"See you tomorrow," I said to Shelby when the bus stopped at my house.

"See you tomorrow! Hope you like it."

"Hope I like what?"

"You'll find out," she said smiling and waving me on to get off of the bus.

Grandma was in the living room when I walked into the house.

"Come in here, Helen," she said. "I've got a surprise for you."

"What is it Grandma?"

"You'll see," she answered with a big smile on her face. "You can bring it in, Henry."

Grandpa came into the living room dancing on his tiptoes. He was holding a cardboard box up above his head; twirling and swaying side to side.

"I've got a surpri-i-ise," he sang. "I've got a surpri-i-se." He laid the box at my feet. A soft meowing sound came out of the box as I opened the lid.

"It's a kitten!" I said excitedly. I reached into the box and pulled out a little white kitten and sat it on my lap.

"She's was from one of Mama Cat's latest litters," Grandma said. "Shelby helped me pick out the liveliest one."

"But you don't like cats."

"Oh, I like cats. It was Daisy who didn't like cats."

"Is she mine?"

"She's all yours," Grandpa replied. "We thought it might help if you had something to take care of and to love."

"Thank you, Grandma and Grandpa," I said hugging them around the neck.

"I called your Grandma and Grandpa Roy and asked them if you could take a pet home for the summer, because it's going to be your responsibility to feed it and take care of it," Grandma said. "They thought that was a wonderful idea. Your grandma said something about having someone named Mary Lou make a red, white, and blue outfit for it and putting it in the Fourth of July parade this summer."

"That's my grandma's best friend. One year she dressed up her little terrier in an Uncle Sam outfit, and he walked on his hind legs during most of the parade."

"Well, she also said to tell you she misses you, and she and your grandpa love you very much. This hug and kiss are from them." Then Grandma hugged me and kissed me on the cheek.

"What are you going to call her?" Grandpa asked. "A name has to be something special, something the critter can live up to."

"I'm going to call her Hope, Grandpa, because this afternoon, I feel like life is worth living if you have people who love you."

Then Grandma hugged me and started crying again.

"Don't cry, Grandma," I said patting her arm.

"I'm just crying because I'm happy," she said wiping her eyes. "That's the best name you could have given her, Helen."

Then Grandpa and I said at the same time, "It's Lizzy, Grandma. It's Lizzy." She looked at us, eyes wide with surprise, and the three of us burst out laughing,

Just then the phone rang and Grandpa answered it.

"Marjorie? Is it really you?"

Grandma's face had a questioning look as she hurried over to the phone.

"Is it our Marjorie, Henry?" she asked Grandpa.

Grandpa shook his head yes and Grandma sat down at the dining room table like her legs couldn't hold her up anymore. I put the kitten in the box and walked over to her side just as Grandpa was hanging up the phone.

He turned to Grandma and me and said, "Marjorie wants to come home."

CHAPTER 27

We borrowed Uncle Don's station wagon to pick up my mom from the train station. We rode there in silence, each one of us with our own thoughts of what this reunion would be like. I pictured it in my mind, but I was unprepared for the way my mother looked when I saw her. It was such a contrast to the way she appeared six months earlier when she dropped me off with my ticket to come to Tennessee. Then she was dressed in the latest fashion with her nails polished and her high heeled shoes shining. She was full of confidence that she would be a star as soon as she hit New York City. Now it looked like New York City had hit her and hard at that. Her peasant top and long skirt were shabby and needed washing. Her long straight hair had been dyed a dirty blond and was matted like it hadn't been combed in days. Long beads hung around her neck down to her thin waist.

So this is what a hippie looks like, I thought as Grandma and Grandpa hugged and kissed her.

"I've made such a wreck of my life, Daddy," she cried into Grandpa's shoulder. "Can you ever forgive me? Can God ever forgive me?"

"You're our daughter," Grandpa said. "You were lost, but now you are found, Marjorie. God forgives you and so do we."

Grandma couldn't say anything. She just cried and held her prodigal daughter like she'd never let her go again.

Grandma is getting her prayers answered, I thought. But I didn't know about the "we" part of Grandpa's statement. I wasn't ready to forgive and forget. I had been hurt too badly to kiss and make up that easily. Even though I had spent the last day and a half anticipating her return and going over things I would say to my mother, I was speechless when the time actually came.

"Lizzy, I am so sorry," Mom said drawing me into her arms. "I've been such a fool. I almost lost the most important person in my life. I love you, Lizzy. Please forgive me."

Years of resentment melted at those simple words, "forgive me." Wasn't that what it was all about, forgiveness? Words of Grandpa's sermons came back to me. "If you do not forgive others, God will not forgive you. Jesus came to seek and find the lost, to forgive them of their sins," he had said. "If he can forgive them, we can forgive them too with his help."

"Yes," I said looking up at her. "I forgive you."

Later after she'd had a bath and rested, Mom told us how a letter from a lawyer telling her of Dad's death, had awakened her to how she was destroying her life with alcohol and wild living.

"I took a good look at myself and saw how far I had fallen from God's grace," Mom said. "I fell on my knees and begged God to forgive me and help me straighten out my life. All I could think of for days was to call home, but I was afraid you wouldn't want me back. Thank you. Thank you for letting me come home."

"You can stay here for as long as you want, Marjorie," Grandpa told her, "But you need to make some changes. Ed Harley is coming over this evening to talk to you. He wants to sponsor you in the A.A. program he has been attending, and I think you ought to give it a try."

Mom shook her head, "Yes, Daddy, I'll try it. I know I need help with my drinking. I can't beat this problem by myself. I've tried that before and it is like I am powerless over my desire for alcohol. I haven't had a drink since I got the letter about Jason, but the desire is still there. I could use a stiff drink right now."

"Coffee is the strongest drink you'll be getting in this house," Grandma said as she got up and walked to the kitchen to pour her a cup.

When she came back, Grandma was also carrying a small box. It was the one Grandpa and Grandma Roy had given me after Daddy died. I'd forgotten all about it. I sat down on the couch between Grandma and Mom, and we opened the box. Inside were Daddy's dog tags, his wallet, a cigarette lighter, a small book, and his wedding ring. Mom opened the wallet and there was a picture of her and Daddy when they were first married. There was a laminated newspaper picture of me and Grandma and Grandpa Roy on the Fourth of July when Mary Lou's wig caught on fire. I laughed when I saw the picture of us standing over the smoking cone with shocked looks on our faces. The caption said, "The fireworks start early for some Indianapolis parade goers."

"That probably gave Jason a laugh every time he looked at it," Mom said with tears falling down her face. "I wish I'd been there to see that, Lizzy. I wish I'd been there for you all of your life."

Grandma picked up the little book and opened it.
"What is it?" I asked.

"It's a little New Testament that they must have passed out to the soldiers before they left for Vietnam." Grandma turned to the first page. There were words written in my daddy's handwriting.

"Listen to this," she said and began to read what daddy had written.

> "I gave my life to Jesus Christ and was baptized on October 17, 1966. Maggie and Lizzy, I'm sorry I've made such a mess of my life. Jesus is helping me get it back together. I hope someday you can forgive me for ever running out on the two of you. I love you both so much.
>
> Love, Jason."

Now tears were coming from all of our eyes. I wiped my nose on Grandma's apron and turned to Grandpa.

"Grandpa, I've been thinking about this for a long time. I want to be baptized too."

"Oh, Helen!" Grandma said. "That's another prayer God has answered for me today."

"You can call her Lizzy, Mom," my mother said.

"That's okay, Grandma, you can call me what ever you want." Then I turned to my mom. "The kids at school call me Helen all the time because my teacher tells them to. I'll never be Lizzy there."

"Well, when I get on my feet, I'll have a little talk with your teacher," Mom said. "I know Mrs. Higgins. She used to like me when I was in the 5th grade. I think there'll be some changes coming soon."

"The best change has already come," I said smiling up at her. And then I knew it was true what Grandma had said about God answering prayers. He hadn't been telling me, "No," when I'd asked him to bring my mom back. He'd only been saying to wait, and today, he finally said, "Yes."